HEARTTHROB
A Lovers' Heart Series

Cheryl Barton

Published by Barton Publishing, LLC

Cheryl Barton
P.O. Box 962
Reisterstown, Maryland 21136
http://www.cherylbarton.net

Ordering Information:
Quantity sales. Special discounts are available on quantity purchases by corporations, associations, and others. For details, contact the publisher at the address above.

Orders by U.S. trade bookstores and wholesalers. Please contact cheryl@cherylbarton.net

ISBN: 0692418334
ISBN-13: 978-0692418338

To my friends who love reading and experiencing love, I want to thank you for your support and your friendship!

I am because you read - Cheryl

Connect with me

Visit my website at www.CherylBarton.net
Twitter – @Author Cheryl Barton
Instagram – AuthorCherylBarton
Facebook at Author Cheryl Barton
Email – Cheryl@CherylBarton.net
Blog - https://mswriterinmd.wordpress.com/

ABOUT HEARTTHROB

Cade Weston, Hollywood's most eligible bachelor and named the world's sexiest man of the year, lives life at the top with a bevy of beauties at his beck and call, people providing his every desire and more money than any one person can spend in a lifetime.

Callie Hurston struggles to make it as a stylist to the stars in a world where women are intimidated by her beauty and men are interested in her body and not her talent.

Cade thought he had it all until he has a chance meeting with Callie and decides to take a chance on her talent and ends up taking an even bigger chance with his heart.

Can the playboy turn in his player's card and give in to love?

Other Romance Novels by Cheryl Barton

Bachelor Series

Bachelor Not For Sale
A Designed Affair
A Perfect Combination
Love at Last – Coming Fall 2015
Twelve Bachelors For Sale – Coming 2016

Amorous Occupations Series

The Artist
The Bookkeeper
The Chef
The Dancer
The Electrician – Coming August 2015
The Flight Attendant – Coming Early 2016

Inspirational

Down, But Not Out: Breaking Chains
A Purpose-Filled Dash: Living an Empire State of Mind

Inspirational Compilations

One Sister Away: Encouraging Words From One Sister
to Another, Volume 1
One Sister Away: Encouraging Words From One Sister
to Another, Volume 2
A Letter to My Mother

Stand Alone Romance Novels

Holly For Christmas
Second Chances: Three Valentine Novellas
Bossy – Coming Summer 2015
Un-break My Heart – Coming Winter 2015
Heartbeat – Coming Early 2016

Dear Reader,

I hope you enjoy Cade and Callie's story. Each day we experience hot fantasies about heartthrobs we see on television and movie screens. Today, I'm bringing you that hotness within the pages of this romance novel.

Cade's story is the first of three in my new series, *A Lovers' Heart Series* and I hope you enjoy them all with satisfying delight. First up is *Heartthrob*, followed by *Heartbeat* in early 2016 and closing out the series is *Heartbreaker* later in 2016.

I loved writing *Heartthrob* and I thoroughly enjoyed letting my imagination about hot sexy men take me away. Think about that man that makes your heart race and then sit back and enjoy everything that is Cade Weston!

Happy Reading!

Cheryl Barton

Prologue

"Mr. Weston, can I get a moment of your time?" a voice shouted.

"Cade! Over here please," another voice bellowed in the crowd.

"Cade, what was the most challenging aspect of your most recent film?" a male shouted over all the other voices.

"What do you like most about being Cade Weston, being an actor, running your own record label, having a successful apparel line or is it the countless number of women who throw themselves at you daily?" a female voice shrieked.

"Cade, can I have your baby?" That question made him laugh, something else he heard daily.

"Mr. Weston, what's next for you, is it a new movie or a brand new business venture?" another voice hollered.

"Mr. Weston, are you single? I have a daughter and I think she'd be perfect for you!"

Cade smiled as questions were being thrown at him from the crowd that gathered outside of the Los Angeles television station. It was daytime, but he had just wrapped up the taping of his appearance on a late night talk show. He was told to expect the crowd once word got out that he would be there. He expected a crowd, but nothing like what he encountered as he exited the building while his team of security made a path so that he could get into the waiting limousine.

"Cade, what do you think of the nickname everyone has given you, calling you 'Heartthrob'? I hear it's because of the number of broken hearts you leave behind and the throbbing bodies women and some men experience just by getting a glimpse of you?" yet another voice shouted.

Cade stopped in his tracks at hearing himself being called heartthrob.

Recently, that pseudonym had been plastered on the cover of every magazine and news story written about him. He liked it, especially when people tried to define the title with their own characterization. He found it hilarious each time he read a new story about him and his sexual prowess, something that kept his name in the headlines.

"You don't have time to stop and answer questions Cade," Abby, his personal assistant said, urging him to keep walking.

Cade knew she was right and though he was tempted to answer some of the questions, he continued on to the limousine and got in followed by Abby and Aaron, his chief of security.

"That is some crowd, especially this early in the morning," Aaron said.

Aaron was not only Cade's chief of security, but also one of his best friends since their college days.

"It is and I am who I am because of crowds like that."

"I see this heartthrob thing isn't going away. I'm beginning to think you're enjoying the title, brother."

Cade didn't answer, but gave his friend a slick smile. Being labeled a heartthrob and plastered on the cover of magazines certainly had its benefits.

"What's on the agenda for today?" Aaron asked.

"I'm going home to work out and then I believe I have several meetings at the record label. My artists are climbing the charts and because of that, we've been getting in demos from aspiring artists from around the world. There are a few my team who is responsible for new talent want me to hear. Then, later tonight, I'm going to be eye candy on the arm of Ms. Diamond at a fundraising event. Does that about cover it Abby?" he asked turning toward her and making sure he hadn't left anything out. He noticed she had yet to lift her head from her cell phone no doubt booking him for another public appearance somewhere. He didn't question her; he just followed along.

"That's pretty much it. You asked me to clear your calendar after the event with Ms. Diamond tonight."

Aaron knew what that meant. Cade was often called on to accompany some of the most beautiful women in the world to events to keep the buzz about them in the media. He knew that Cade believed that all press was good press in Hollywood. He had, after all, recently been name the sexiest man on the planet. Everyone wanted to be seen with him and all women wanted to get under him, literally. Aaron had a feeling Diamond would be engaging in both before the evening was over.

"Abby, can you get my usual suite ready for tonight and since I'll be entertaining, roll out the usual including my staple gift. Check to be sure it's not one that I've given Diamond in the past."

"Do you want me to add flowers this time as well?" she inquired.

Cade thought about it and knew it wouldn't be necessary with Diamond.

"No flowers tonight, but make sure my driver sticks around since she won't be staying all night." Abby didn't respond or even react since they were all accustomed to Cade's penchant for entertaining and then moving on. This was going to be one of those nights. He would be doing his part to keep Diamond in the spotlight by being seen with her and in turn, she would spend the evening in whatever way he chose.   He was Cade Weston, media mogul, box office smash, actor and of course, according to the entertainment world, 'heartthrob' and he planned on living up to that name tonight.

1

Cade groaned as the piercing shrill of the ringing phone continued to pull him from a deep slumber. After the night he was now recollecting as he slowly came awake, it was an unwelcomed sound caused by sheer exhaustion. He tried to call on the sleep that was beginning to elude him, knowing the hour of the day was early and the sleep he had already indulged in hadn't lasted long enough. This is the life that he worked hard for, he thought, until phones rang out for him when he didn't want them to at ungodly hours of the morning like now. It was times like this that he would gladly give up his life for a few extra hours of uninterrupted siesta.

The phone continued to ring as he refused to open his eyes or even move for fear that he would have to get up and start the day earlier than he'd planned. He'd gotten in late the night before and hours after, he was still wide awake, enjoying the celebrity status he'd come to love. A smarter man would have turned off his own phone and had the hotel hold all of his calls until a more decent hour, like twelve noon. He had been too wrapped up in his evening of pleasure and any thoughts of phones or any other disturbances were the furthest from his mind.

As the ringing stopped, he forced his mind to take him back to that place where he didn't have to worry about the person calling, who he was sure wanted something from him because everyone around him did. He was, after all, Cade Weston, the most sought after celebrity in the world and everyone wanted a piece of him. He was blessed to be him, but at the moment, it actually sucked.

The day was starting out to be the kind of day where he wished he was someone else other than Cade Weston. The Cade Weston he was had endless appointments that included going over new movie projects, going over scripts for a new television show he was producing, to approving new designs for his men's clothing and cologne lines. Then there were the countless number of appearances he made where paparazzi never gave him a break, but instead followed his every move, reporting on his every action, which sometimes included him merely drinking a cup of coffee at a bistro reading the newspaper. There was nothing exciting about that, but because he was Cade Weston, people around the world were interested.

One of his most profitable businesses was his record label, Covert Entertainment. His label was the hottest in town and his roster of artists was being compared to the launch of Motown many years ago at a time when they released music by artists that topped the charts over any other record label in the country. Everything he touched seemed to turn to platinum. This, he knew, was the life of Cade Weston, mogul-extraordinaire.

He was no slouch when it came to the entertainment industry, especially with his last four films all reaching number one at the box office. He was at the top of everyone's list and it appeared that someone had no problem calling on him before the sun rose in the morning.

The ringing phone broke into thoughts of his successes, as what started out as the sound of his ringing cell phone turned into the ringing of the phone in the suite which sounded like someone was ringing the bell on top of a church and as loud as it sounded, he felt like he was standing right next to it as it was being rung.

He wanted to cover his ears with his hands to drown out the sound as he willed it to go away, but he couldn't move any part of his body. With the lack of sleep he received and the activities from the night before, he could barely feel his body at all. He'd had the kind of workout that most men only dream about, but because he was Cade Weston, all of his dreams were quickly turned into reality at the snap of his fingers.

"This had better be important," he roared as he rolled to his left in the king sized bed of the penthouse suite of the hotel to search for and destroy the ringing phone.

What he encountered as he turned blocked his reach as he rolled into something soft and luscious. He felt that lusciousness and it wiggled under his touch. Hearing the ringing again, which now appeared to be coming from the opposite direction of his reach, he rolled the other way and had the same encounter with another something soft and luscious. He couldn't stop the smile that gradually appeared on his face even if he wanted to knowing that those were not bed pillows on either side of him. He continued to smile as images of the night before flashed across his mind and the last thing he wanted to do was move.

He received no reprieve from the phone so he came fully awake, turned over and sat up, looking to his left and to his right at the two sleeping forms. He knew he didn't have to look to know that they were probably naked under the blanket, but he couldn't help himself and looked anyway. Sure enough, both women were naked and snoring from what he knew was enervation. They had enjoyed quite an evening together and before he knew it, that part of him that kept him in trouble with the ladies came wide awake, causing a tent to form over that part of him that was still covered by the blanket. It appeared his body was ready for a repeat of the night before. Images of bodies smacking, bouncing and rolling all over the bed clouded his mind as his body hardened even more.

He thought back to the activities of the night before and remembered how he ended up with the two beauties.

He had traveled to New York from his home-base in California to attend a meeting to test samples of his new men's cologne, the latest in his launch of businesses that will add to the millions he had already acquired in his thirty-one years of life.

After his meeting wrapped, he selected the one he wanted that made him think of what the ladies would love to smell on their man. He then agreed to make an appearance at the opening of one of his friends' Luke's night club called Estopia. The club was being touted as the hottest club in the New York area and the fact that due to the high demand of celebrities wanting to get in, there was no room for guests who were not on the list prior to the opening.

Everyone who was anyone was in attendance and he had to admit it was one of the best times he'd had out in a long time. He was known for his partying ways, but he pretty much kept that to the west coast. He was constantly hounded by paparazzi, but that was something he had adapted to and it had gotten worse after he'd recently been named the sexiest man in the world by the number one celebrity magazine that everyone picked up each month. With him and his penetrating hazel eyes and sexy stance, the magazine broke records in sales the month he was on the cover. He appreciated the honor, but not the additional attention and spotlight on every move he made and every word that came out of his mouth.

He'd had to hire additional public relations staff to help deal with the extra attention and requests for his time. Attending the opening of the club was something he would never miss and after a stressful day of meetings, he had been ready for the fun and relaxation. He ordered his favorite bottle of liquor and sat back and waited for the night to really jump off.

He'd had his bodyguards on full alert the entire evening, knowing he would be hounded by everyone for attention and the night didn't disappoint.

Semi-successful actors and music artists wanted his attention to either lend them a hand getting an acting gig or adding them as a new artist on his record label.

The women flashed smiles and other body parts to try and turn his attention their way which was something he was met with daily, so it was no surprise to him.

There was a plethora of women around to satisfy whatever need he had and last night, after having more drinks than he should have consumed, taking away his ability to think clearly, he'd pointed out one of the sexiest women in the room and sent a member of his loyal entourage over to ask her to join him in his exclusive VIP section of the club. The woman made it known she was not alone and if she came, her friend had to join them and after getting a glimpse of the friend who was just as sexy as she was, Cade willingly accepted the offer for them both to join him.

Women were his weakness and having every magazine, newspaper and internet site boast reminders that he was very single, he only had to give a signal and women were all over him. He loved and craved the attention as any other man in his position would do. He was amazed, yet not surprised, at the offers he got from ladies on a regular basis. His expertise in bed when it came to pleasing a woman was well talked about and publicized and every story was printed the same way, stating that no one ever left his bed unsatisfied.

Every woman wanted to be the one woman who finally tame him as if they had something that made him want to give up being a bachelor. Time after time, he proved to them all that there wasn't a woman alive who could tame Cade Weston. He'd dated more women than he could count, but none ever had what he would be looking for if he were interested in anything exclusive, which he was not.

He had yet to encounter anyone, male or female who didn't have an ulterior motive for wanting to be around him or to be considered his friend and so he relegated himself to the fact that he would probably remain single and he was okay with that. He'd dated models, actresses, politicians and none had anything special that made him want anything exclusive. He wasn't called 'The Playboy' for nothing. He was living the life most people dreamed about and he wouldn't want to exchange it for anything; not even if there was such a thing as the perfect woman for him.

After partying and drinking for hours, he left the club with the two women in tow and headed straight for the penthouse suite at one of his favorite New York hotels. He decided to not stay at the condo he'd recently purchased in New York for when he was in town on business, choosing to never take a woman there. That was his private sanctuary whenever he came to New York and it was a place where he had never taken a woman, preferring to keep his rendezvous to hotels where the next day, they could all walk away and his private domain wouldn't be violated with unexpected pictures being taken or other personal things disappearing.

After arriving at the hotel, he dismissed his security detail for the evening and he and the two women partied the rest of the night in his room where they showed him that two was definitely better than one; something they showed him over and over again and in countless ways and positions all night long.

Both were sexy like he liked his women and once they found out he was in the club, he had no doubt they ramped their sexiness up to a whole new level to get noticed and notice he did.

Once they were locked inside of his penthouse suite, it didn't take long for them to drop every stitch of clothing showing him how real every part of their bodies were. He also remembered feasting on their succulent bodies as they in turn, returned the favor, leaving no spot on his body that their lips had not ventured to.

Now here he was, in the light of what he knew was barely daytime and as usual, he was ready for another round, but he also knew that he was ready for them to leave. He hated allowing women to overstay their welcome. That always led to them thinking there was more to their time together than an exchange of an evening of enjoyable sex.

He loved what all of his fame and fortune brought him, but the morning after always came with regrets.

His regret wasn't in the night he spent being pleasured beyond what he could have ever imagined, but it was how he felt in the morning. He never shared his deepest feelings with anyone because he wanted to continue with the image that his lifestyle was exactly what he wanted, but if he was honest with himself, he would admit that instead of waking up to different women in his bed all the time, one day he'd like to wake up to a woman that he wouldn't want to leave in the light of day.

His cell phone rang again pulling him from thoughts of the night before as the two beauties began to stir and this time he reached across and grabbed it from the night stand before it stopped.

"Yes Abby!" he shouted into the phone.

Only his assistant would call this early and be this persistent to go back and forth between ringing his cell phone and ringing the phone in the suite. He couldn't think of anyone else who would even dare to try it without thinking first of the mayhem he would bring to their life.

"Cade, where are you and why aren't you on your way to the airport? I sent you the information on your next meeting which is back in California today. Don't you tire of always being late?" she asked.

He listened as another barrage of questions were thrown at him before he began tuning out her squeaky voice.

Abby Myers had been his assistant for ten years and she was more like his everything when it came to business. She kept his life in line and he never had to worry about anything. She was like a mother, an assistant and a boss all wrapped up in a tiny, little complete package. At only five feet, three inches tall, she was a powerhouse that was not to be messed with. The way she could cut her eyes when she was angry would silence the strongest of men.

Cade rubbed the sleep from his eyes and drew his hand down across his jaw then down to his chest as he patiently waited for her bombardment of his whereabouts to stop.

"Abby, it's a little early for twenty questions. My head is pounding and right now the last thing I'm thinking about is the airport and a business meeting."

Cade looked on as two sets of the plumpest breasts he'd ever been this close to came even closer, apparently with the same thought in their minds as he had in his, which was one last round for the road. Thoughts of escorting them to the door was the furthest from his mind as his body hardened to a point of painful arousal with a touch of enjoyment of what was about to be in store for him. He smiled as he looked down to where his engorged member stood at attention, never disappointing him with its readiness to get the job done.

"Cade, I'm serious, this is no time for foolishness and whatever woman you have buried in that bed with you, you need to get rid of her and get to the airport right now. Remember, you have the number one basketball player in the country about to sign a deal to endorse your new line of footwear. I don't think you want to miss this meeting and the press that will be all over it. Pre-sales alone have topped the sales of the biggest brand out these days, so try not to screw this up by showing up unfashionably late. This will be big for you and for *Cadence* your women's fragrance line and *Cado*, the new men's cologne. Get your ass out of that bed, away from the woman or women I know you're probably wrapped around, get dressed and get to the airport. Your private jet will get you out of New York and back to the west coast just in time to make your meeting."

Cade heard her, but he wasn't listening. Right now his body and mind had other things it was considering that had nothing to do with getting out of bed. He felt two sets of hands traveling across his body, going up and down across his six-pack and heading further south. He needed to get Abby off the phone before she hears more than he wants her to hear.

"Abby, you worry too much and I tell you all the time, stop acting like an old mother hen. You're my assistant so I expect you to handle your end of things and I'll take care of my end."

Cade heard her hiss into the phone, knowing she was losing patience with him as she often did.

"It's your end of things that I'm always worried about Cade. The end that you're thinking with right now is the end that keeps you in trouble, so put it away, back away from the woman and get your ass in gear. You know you make the worse mistakes when you are thinking with the wrong head and usually at this hour, it's that wrong head that I'm always worried about. I'm not going to give you the speech I usually give you so do the right thing here."

"I hear you Abby."

"When you're done placing that wrong head in all the wrong places, get to the airport. I can't reschedule this press conference and contract signing, so please stop making my job hard and help me while I continue to make you an even richer man. This is my last warning Cade, so step away from whoever you have sprawled out across your bed right now and get to the airport. Why must we have this conversation every morning? You know what your schedule looks like and what it takes for me to juggle everything to keep you on track. I'm surprised your penis hasn't completed given out on you yet as much as you whip it out. Work with me by doing me this solid and get up. There is a lot riding on this deal and you know what it took to get this together."

"Hey, I've told you before. You are never to talk about my penis under any circumstances. It doesn't sound right coming from you and I said I'm getting up and I am," he chortled.

Cade paused in his attempt to show the roaming hands what he wanted them to do. Abby was right and he needed to focus and the best way to do that and get back to handling his business was to first clear his suite and then get his ass to the airport to get back to the west coast where plans for increasing his wealth needed to be finalized.

"I hear you and I'll get there on time. Stop worrying your pretty little head about this and focus more on this press conference today. I'm getting up right now and I'll be on the west coast before you can complain again," he cheerfully said, hoping it would ease Abby's frustration with him.

"You also have a production meeting for the television show, there are six new movie roles that you're being offered, one I've already agreed to on your behalf because it's being written and directed by two of your favorites so there is a contract for you to sign on the jet. I'll run the others by you when you get here. There's also some new up and coming model that you're being asked to escort to the biggest fashion event of the year. They are willing to pay you handsomely to have her seen on your arm for publicity since it'll help launch her career and get people talking about her. I've set up a meeting about that this evening and some baseball star who wants to turn into a recording artist wants to meet with you while he's in town tonight. He said you agreed to meet with him as a personal favor for a friend."

He forgot all about that meeting he'd agreed to. Apparently this ball player could also blow as an R&B singer and he wants in on Cade's record label.

"Alright Abby, I'm getting up and I promise I'll be in California and on time for the press conference. We'll talk about everything else when I get there."

"Good and I hope you had fun in New York, but it's time for the playboy to come home. There is a lot to do in the next twenty-four hours alone."

Cade hung up and just when he was about to ignore Abby's rants that were living in his mind and turn to the beauties, there was a knock on the door of the suite. He knew that was Aaron and he had no doubt that as soon as he and Abby disconnected, she'd called him to put a fire under him.

He looked at the lustful glares of two women looking back at him and though he was tempted to ignore everyone but them, he changed to thinking with the right head and got up to escort them out and to get to his waiting jet. He knew an extremely cold shower would be in store for him and that the fun was finally over. It was time for Cade Weston the playboy to cool off and for Cade Weston the business man to step up.

As they all began moving around, he looked from one woman to the other and realized the struggle of what to do was real. He suddenly thought of how he could kill two birds with one stone. He grabbed his cell phone and sent Aaron a text that he'd be out after his shower. He then turned back to two women he didn't want to disappoint.

"Ladies, what do you say to joining me for my morning shower before you leave?"

He smiled as neither said a word, but in all of

their spectacular nakedness they walked toward the adjoining bathroom.

"I love being Cade Weston," he said turning in the direction of the bathroom to follow them in.

2

Callie paced back and forth in her New York City apartment overlooking Manhattan, angry at herself for thinking that again she would be taken seriously as an entertainment stylist and not looked at as a woman with a motive to get into bed with every male client she worked with.

For the past three years, she'd worked with some of the biggest names in the entertainment industry and though she'd come a long way, she still felt like she hadn't gone anywhere since she first began.

After graduating college she'd landed the biggest contract of her life when a rising R&B artist saw sketches of new designs she'd created and after deciding to go in a new direction and shock the world with a new image, she was hired to be his personal stylist. That job had led to several others and over a year ago she had been hired as the stylist on the set of a hot new reality series based on the lives of up and coming artists in New York.

Her life had been bliss until the hottest star on the show, Mateo, developed a reputation for bedding every woman he came across, including those he worked with. In the midst of all of his bedding, he proposed to Asia, a beautiful starlet on the series and though Asia had known her from the beginning of the show and they had actually become friends, once Asia was engaged to Mateo, Callie noticed a change in how Asia dealt with her.

On the set, Asia made remarks about how close Callie had to be when measuring and styling Mateo and it began causing a problem. She thought back to the heated conversation with Asia a few days before she had been fired from the set.

She'd gone to Asia's dressing room to ask her about rumors she'd been hearing about liaisons with Mateo that were not true.

"Asia, can I speak to you for a minute please?" Callie asked after her after she answered the door to her dressing room.

Callie knew something was up when Asia wouldn't look her in the face, but waved her into the room. She entered and closed the door behind her not wanting anyone walking by to hear their conversation.

"You have five minutes Callie," Asia said turning her back to her.

"Did I do something to you? I thought we were cool, but getting the cold shoulder from you a lot lately says otherwise. I thought we could talk about whatever the problem is and move beyond it."

She stepped back a little when Asia turned around to face her with fiery eyes and body language that said she was ready for a fight.

"Don't come in here trying to act all innocent as if you care anything about me or whatever friendship we had."

Callie noticed she'd said 'had' when she mentioned their friendship. She remained calm knowing coming back at her with anger would only add fuel to the situation and she came in to resolve a problem, not create one.

"Why don't you tell me what I did and get whatever issues we have resolved? I'm hearing a lot of rumors and if what I'm hearing has anything to do with why you're upset with me, I can tell you that they aren't true."

She watched as Asia stopped fooling with her hair and stiffened, still not turning around.

"I figured you'd say that, but I'm being told differently. I hear you've been seen coming out of Mateo's hotel room late at night during our off days. I've heard that before he and I became engaged that you were his play thing and styling him isn't the only thing you do for him on your knees. I know Mateo and his hankering for the ladies, but now that we're engaged whatever you two have going on is totally disrespectful to me. I don't blame him because he's a man and it's what men do when women hand them sex on a silver platter. I see why he likes you with your exotic looks. You're a beautiful woman and any woman would kill for a natural body like yours that doesn't need any cosmetic enhancements. You walk around here with your killer looks and killer body and I see every head turn when you walk by and not just the men either. How many others besides Mateo have you serviced to get and keep your job?"

She was hurt hearing the vile that was spewing from Asia's mouth and she wouldn't take being called a whore by her or any other person. Though she was hurt by the accusation, she kept her cool when she spoke.

"None of that is true. I have never been with Mateo in an intimate way and no one else around here can say that I have been with them either. I am a professional at all times, even when I see members of the crew when I'm out and around New York during my downtime. Mateo and I have never had any kind of a relationship other than a professional one. Don't try to insult me by belittling me as if only my looks got me this job. I come with intelligence as well, though only small minds wouldn't recognize that."

Callie could feel her anger getting the best of her and this wasn't what she came in here for.

Asia did turn around when she realized the insult that came with her words. She could see that Asia was angry, but the sinister look accompanied by the smile that crept on her face was almost frightening.

Asia smiled at her like Callie's words were going in one ear and out of the other, not sinking in.

"Who said anything about a relationship? I'm talking about sex to get ahead. Isn't that how women in your line of work make it in this industry? No one takes your talent for style and fashion seriously. It's what's under all that style and fashion that they're interested in."

Callie paused before responding, trying to hold her flaring temper down.

"I don't know what you've heard or how those rumors got started, but I'm telling you none of it is true. You've known me from the start of the show and not once have you ever seen me with anyone or given anyone the impression that I'm that type of person because I'm not."

"Well from what I hear, you are that type of person. I think I heard something about you being involved with an artist you were styling a few years ago. For someone who's not like that, you were like that then. I'm supposed to believe, given the opportunity to snag Mateo who is about to blow up, you wouldn't?"

She hated when her past came back to haunt her. When she first started out as a stylist, she had gotten involved with one of the artist she was working with, but to her they were in a relationship and it wasn't something casual. She had no idea he wasn't thinking the same way. She acquired a label for bedding her artists, though it was only one and yet it still followed her around several years later. Now at the age of twenty-eight, she was still dealing with the same mess, though now, it's without cause.

"That was a long time ago and the circumstances were different. We were in a relationship and not hiding that we were seeing each other."

"Yeah, well I don't want you thinking you're going to snag Mateo from under me. I'm riding that train all the way to the top even if it means I'll need to get a few enhancements in order to compete with women who look like you naturally with big breasts and a J-Lo behind, the way I know Mateo loves his women to look."

Callie didn't want to sound like she was pleading or begging for understanding, but she thought that the friendship they had developed was honest enough that she wouldn't believe such disgusting rumors. Apparently she was wrong.

"I'm not now nor have I been interested in Mateo and I'm not involved with him in any way other than professionally as his stylist. We have never been intimate. I know how much you love Mateo and he loves you."

She watched as Asia stood as if to signal that their conversation was over.

"I see that you are trying to make me feel better about all of this, but I see how he looks at you. He wants you and there is nothing I can do about it if he decides to make a play for you."

Callie was tiring of the conversation. It was insecure women in this business like Asia that could have a negative impact on a career like hers and she wasn't going to let her or any other woman make her out to be a tramp just to placate their own insecurities.

"I decide who I get involved with and I can't help that men find me attractive. I love the career I've chosen and I've always been about my business and nothing else. Any ideas you have of anything else is a figment of your imagination and anyone else's who has decided to spread nasty rumors about me."

Callie watched as Asia nonchalantly went about flipping her hair and straightening her clothes as if the conversation was a waste of her time.

"Please save that for someone who really cares because I don't. All I know is what I see and what I see is a woman who has a history of messing around with the men she works with and I also know that Mateo is fine in every way and can have any woman he wants and from where I sit, he wants you."

"Anyone wanting me doesn't mean I'm returning that interest. There is no way I can do anything about someone who finds me attractive. I know myself and I know that I don't mess around where I work and like I said before, I have been nothing but professional since I've started here. Are you really this insecure to think that because Mateo may find me attractive that he'll get me because he wants me and that would what, leave you out in the cold? I'm not trying to ride the Mateo train anywhere. I'm here to work and that's all. If you and Mateo are having issues with other women, I suggest you look around a little more because on this set, I'm not who you should be worried about. There are knees around here that have lots of carpet burns courtesy of Mateo, but I'm not one of them."

She knew she'd gone too far as Asia clenched her fists and her face showed rage.

"Get out!" Asia shouted.

She hadn't meant to hit below the belt and tried to apologize.

"Asia, look I'm sorry and I didn't mean to say that to you. We have had a cordial relationship this whole time, yet I don't know how things have gotten to this point, but I had no right to say what I said and I'm sorry. I am no threat to what you and Mateo have going on."

"Threat? You think you're a threat to me? You're not a threat, but you can become a distraction and any distraction could get in the way of what I have planned for my life and that life consists of Mateo. One day he's going to be big and I plan to be on his arm."

She was beginning to tire of explaining herself when clearly Asia had already made up her mind that the rumors floating around were true.

"Like I said, I'm not the distraction you should be worried about. He's already distracted and I'm not the cause of it because he may look my way, but I'm not looking his way."

"Get out Callie," Asia said before she turned towards the back of her dressing room, dismissing her again.

She didn't want to fuel the fire anymore, so she turned to leave.

Thinking back on that day two weeks ago and the conversation that led to her current unemployment status angered her. When nothing happened in the few days after their argument, she'd assumed everything was water under the bridge, though she could tell Asia watched her carefully whenever Mateo was around. However, when she'd arrived on the set of the show three days ago as she did each morning, she was told her services were no longer needed. After their conversation, apparently Asia had approached Mateo about Callie's accusations about him and other women on the set and it had set off a storm of controversy that she wasn't aware of. Mateo no longer wanted her styling him because of all the dirt that came out about several women around the set that he'd actually been intimate with even after proposing to Asia. Though he and Asia had worked things out, neither wanted her around anymore so she was out of a job.

Callie hadn't been too worried about losing that job though it paid very well. Her worry came with another job she'd had where she was also let go as a result of what happened on the reality show. Word had gotten out about the controversy on the set and her involvement and it began impacting another opportunity she was given.

One of her biggest clients, a professional basketball player who played for the New York team terminated her contract two days ago. It seems his new wife had heard about the one incident in Callie's past as well as the issue surrounding her leaving the reality show and decided she didn't want Callie around her man either. According to his wife, she didn't want a woman as beautiful as Callie tempting her husband, especially when he was on the road and she couldn't keep her eye on Callie.

She had never been more embarrassed in her life. She'd made one mistake years ago and now it was being used against her when it came to work. The artist she had been styling back then that she did get involved with wasn't married or seeing anyone so they were both free to see each other. He was focused on his career and unbeknownst to her, not interested in a relationship and when others found out they were seeing each other, he brushed it off as something casual to pass the time. To say she was embarrassed was an understatement. She should have known better because he was one of the biggest rising stars in the hip-hop community and thinking he would pass up all other women for her had been a dream on her end. She thought he was a nice guy, but he turned out to be a player. She'd learned her lesson and since then had kept her work and personal lives separate. She now realized that didn't seem to help years later.

Maybe it was time to get out of New York she thought. She had an interview set up in California that she was heading to on an afternoon flight. If she got that job, perhaps she could have a new start and put New York and all of its drama behind her.

She stopped pacing after going over the mess with Asia in her head and returned to packing for her trip. Somewhere on her bed her cell phone was ringing and she dug through the mounds of clothes to find it. It was her mother.

"Hey mom," she said answering cheerfully to not let on that all hell was breaking loose in her life.

"Callie, honey, I've been calling you since yesterday. You know how I worry when you don't answer or call me back. I was concerned when you told me what happened with your jobs even though I know you're keeping most of the details from me. Are you okay?"

She sat down on the edge of her bed relaxing to the sound of her mother's voice. Her mother always knew the right time to call so that she could hear her voice. Sometimes, that was all she needed.

"Mom, I'm fine. Things like this happen in the entertainment industry and I have to learn how to brush it off and move on. I'm actually flying out to California today for an interview on the set of this new television show. The lead actress on the show is also interested in hiring me as her personal stylist and the pay is better than both of the jobs I've had here in New York so don't worry. I'm always going to pick myself up and keep it moving. I can't let other people's insecurities keep me from a career I love so much. This career is just the step I'm going to need in launching my own clothing line so I won't let any setback keep me down while I continue to work out my plan for success as a designer."

"That's good to hear honey, but California? That's such a big town with a reputation for even more drama and mess than New York. Are you sure you want to do that? You know you can always come back home and have a lucrative business as an interior designer. The real estate company could use you to stage all of our homes for sale. I know your line of work is in clothing design, but think of how successful you could be back here in Texas as an interior designer. You would already have lots of connections through your father's real estate business."

Her mom never missed an opportunity to try and coax her back to Texas and out of the entertainment business. She hated the hustle and bustle Callie had to endure to make a living.

"Mom, I love you and I appreciate you always looking out for me, but I don't want to stage homes or do interior design. I want to have my own fashion line and in order to one day do that, I have to stay connected to what the hottest people in the entertainment world are wearing and I can only do that if I am where they are and right now that means going to California."

She heard her mother's inpatient sigh on the other end of the phone and ignored it. She wouldn't be swayed by her mother's desire to have her close. Her parents had their lives and she wanted hers the way she wanted it; on her own terms, doing things her way.

"Ok, I understand. What about money? How are you surviving? Do you need me to wire you some money?"

That made her smile. Her parents were always trying to give her money even when she didn't need it. She was their baby girl and she knew they were always going to look out for her.

"Mom, I have plenty of money saved up. I know it's hard for you to digest, but I make a lot of money as a stylist to the rich and famous, so don't worry. I'm far from destitute and because I was under contract for the rest of this year and next year to style the actors on the show, they had to buy out my contract and pay me for the remainder of it. I'm more than fine with that. If they want to appease their leading actors on the show by getting rid of me, I'm fine with that because I still got paid since the show had been renewed for the next two seasons. I'm glad I signed that new contract earlier this year."

"I'm glad to hear that. What about that other job?"

"They had to pay me through the end of this year as well. My contract to style this athlete was for one year and that had just been renewed four months ago so they had to pay me for the remaining eight months. I know to sign iron-clad contracts so I'm good. With the kind of money he makes, that was pennies to them. I promise you I'm good mom, don't worry. I will call you and dad when I get to California. Angel is even going to fly out to California for a few days to hang with me before I return to New York so I won't be alone. I know that was the next thing you were going to say."

"I'm just glad you're not letting all of this mess get to you. I'm proud of you and so is your dad. I heard Angel got engaged and is planning on getting married next year."

Just when she thought she'd be able to get her mom off of the phone without having the talk about someone's wedding or baby being born, her mom dropped the wedding of her best friend on her which was sure to start a conversation about her own lack of a serious relationship. She did as she always did and let her mother get all of her desires for her daughter to get married and have lots of babies off of her chest.

"Yes, she's coming out not just to visit, but to talk about the plans for the wedding. She wants me to design her dress and the dresses for the bridesmaids. I'm excited for her and DeWayne. They have been together forever and it's about time he popped the question."

"I saw her mother a few days ago and she was happier than I've seen her in years. I'm glad because it was a sad time when Angel's father died a few years ago. This has brightened her spirits a great deal. What time is your flight?"

Callie looked at the phone in shock. Her mother had changed the subject without bringing up marriage and babies, something she never had a problem reminding her that she desired those things for her. She happily went along with the change by checking the time and knew she needed to finish packing.

"In a few hours and I still need to pack."

"Do you want to talk to your father or your sister since I was finally able to catch up with you?"

"No, tell them I said hello and I'll catch up with everyone once I'm in California. I shouldn't be there long, only a few days since the show doesn't start for a few weeks. Styling the lead actress isn't supposed to start for several weeks since it's not for the show, but for her personal appearances. I'm going to fly back here and then I'll stop home in Texas for a few days because if I get this job and the show starts, I won't be able to get home for a few months."

"I'm happy you'll be coming home even if it's

only for a few days. Go on and finish your packing. I don't want to be the cause of you missing your flight. Travel safe and call as soon as you land and check into your hotel."

"I will mom. I love you and tell Dad and Kristine I love them too."

Callie hung up and dashed around her apartment grabbing everything she'd need for her trip to California. She was thankful for the interview and it couldn't have come at a better time. As she moved around, she walked passed her floor to ceiling mirror in her walk in closet and stopped to look at herself. She thought back to her conversation with Asia and though Asia tried to make her feel down about the fact that she was beautiful, she would never do that.

All of her life she'd been complimented on how beautiful she was and how exotic she looked, something she'd gotten from her heritage. Her mom was Filipino and her dad was Puerto Rican and with her darker skin, thick long black hair and what men always called her seductive eyes, she was a beauty. She knew there was no need to deny her looks or to play them down because that would be putting her own self down and that's something she would never do.

As she turned, she glanced at her hour glass figure and knew that she would never apologize to anyone, especially women for not having to enhance her body to feel good about herself. It bothered her that women couldn't be happy with who they were created to be, but if they needed a change, then she was happy if they were happy, but she wouldn't tolerate anyone trying to make her feel bad because she loved who she was inside and out.

She was glad low self-esteem never played a role in her life and even though she has once again encountered another hurdle, she would make her way over this one too and find the greater in her next opportunity.

"You are beautiful," she said to herself in the mirror. "Never forget that your beauty still doesn't define who you are or what you can be. Having beauty is fine, but what you can do is what will project you into the life and career you want, so never settle for less than what you know you are and make sure people respect who you are and not just what you look like."

Callie smiled and walked passed the mirror. It was time to move on to bigger and better.

While she finished packing she called for a taxi service and hoped she'd make it in time for her flight. She didn't want her first impression for the interview to be one of being late.

3

Cade downed his third cup of coffee chasing Tylenol with it to help soothe the effects of his morning sex escape in the shower and of the night before. Too much partying, too much alcohol and a whole lot of sex didn't make for an easy morning of preparing for a flight to California. A smarter man would have reserved his night of partying and taken an earlier flight. He could have partied once he returned home and he would have been in town for his meetings, but he knew he couldn't let his friend down. His appearance brought out the elite for the opening and he was more than happy to help a friend.

The way he was feeling at the moment, he hoped he would survive the trip to the airport.

The night had been a wild one and he knew what it meant to live the life of the number one movie box office draw, pulling in over twenty five million per film, not counting what he took in on the back end from the sales. At the age of thirty-one, that was saying a lot for an actor. There was also talk throughout the Hollywood scene that he would be receiving an Academy nod for his latest film which would put him in even greater demand. His life was a busy one and he chalked it up to the decision he made years ago that this was what he wanted to do.

He had launched a clothing line two years ago and it was one of the top selling lines in the world. Everywhere he went, men were wearing his boxers, his ties, his suits and his custom made brand of shoes.

He was living the good life, but his life hadn't always been this good. He grew up in Compton with two younger brothers and with parents who were both drug addicts. They never had enough food to eat and were teased daily at school because the clothes he and his brothers wore were ragged. His father died from a drug overdose when he was fourteen and his brothers were five and eight years old. When his mother couldn't be located, he and his brothers were placed in temporary foster care for a month until his grandparents flew to California and took them back home with them to Chicago.

Back then, he and his brothers hadn't seen their grandparents in years so the transition from having nothing and never feeling like they were wanted or loved, to moving to Chicago where they were showered with love, affection and all of the things kids should have was a hard one. He, for one, was always looking for the other shoe to drop and they would be snatched from their lives with their grandparents. He was happy it never happened and even though it took over a year, he was finally able to enjoy his new life realizing no one was ever coming to take them away and back to the horrible life they'd had in California. They missed their mom and dad, but they were glad to be out of Compton.

Cade was the oldest so he felt responsible for looking after his baby brothers. His youngest brother Cameron was in college and doing well. His brother Calvin was in the military training to become a navy seal so he wasn't able to hear from him as often as he wanted to, but he heard enough that kept him from worrying. His life was one of secrets, but they were able to stay in contact so that he knew his brother was doing okay. He and Cameron talked often and he had no worries where he was concerned.

He loved his grandparents and when he'd finally made it big in his first starring role at the age of seventeen, he made sure that his grandparents had never wanted for anything ever again. He went home to Chicago to visit them often and times when he could get them to take a break from traveling with their friends, he flew them to visit him in whatever city he was in at the time.

With everyone taken care of, he didn't falter when it came to taking care of his own needs and desires. He had most of what money could buy, including the best cars, more houses than he could live in, money that he'd never be able to spend in a lifetime and the finest women whenever that need arose as well.

He was mister popularity. Anyone could pick up a copy of any of the latest issues of every magazine and he'd be either on the cover or mentioned in one of the stories inside and everyone wanted to know who Cade Weston was linked to. It came with the territory and he knew it.

He checked around his room to be sure he'd gathered everything before calling his team to come in and get his things to the airport. He was about to call Aaron to let him know he was ready when he remembered he was supposed to call his brother back. He needed to check in on him at school to see if he needed anything before he left for California. He knew once he got there, he would be in one business meeting after another.

"Cam, how's it hanging bro?" he asked when Cameron answered.

"Hey, it's hanging just as good as it is for you brother."

"Yeah, well make sure wherever it's hanging, it's layered up two and three times over," he said making reference to what he knew was his brother's overactive sex life.

"You're one to talk. Who is this latest babe I see wrapped around you in the magazines? She's a new one."

"She's nobody and you know it. You should know not to believe all that crap you read in those magazines. I never give interviews on my private life so anything you read is made up to sell them and anything they claim they get first hand from some woman, anyone can make up a story to make a dollar and to help sell magazines. How are classes going? You need anything?"

"Classes are good. College in Florida was the best move I've ever made."

"Ever made? Dude, you're only twenty years old. You haven't made any real moves yet. You know if you need anything to always call Abby. She's been instructed to always take your calls and that any from you and Calvin are a priority."

"Well now that you mention it, I could use an upgrade on my truck."

"No can do on that one. I told you I don't want you being a target and no college student should have a ninety thousand dollar truck. Your truck is fine for what you need it for which is to get you back and forth from your condo to the campus. You have all the luxuries you need at your age so that you don't stand out too much. People know you're my brother and I don't want them trying to get to me through you and for those who don't know, I want it to stay that way as long as possible especially with you being so far away. We've had this conversation many times and you know how I feel about it. When you graduate from graduate school, we'll talk then about any upgrades you need. Until then, I think you're living quite well."

"Are you at least going to let me come to California for the awards show if you get nominated? Can a brother get that?"

He laughed. His brothers didn't ask for much especially with the kind of money he had, but of the two of them, Cameron enjoyed being in the spotlight with him; Calvin could live without it. Luckily, other than those who remember their faces from pictures, once he'd changed his last name from Lymon to Weston when he became an actor, not many people made the connection and his brothers had some semblance of peace and freedom.

"You got that. If I'm nominated, I told you I'd bring you with me. If I could find a way to get Calvin here I'd get a ticket for him too. Have you heard from him lately? Where is he these days?"

"I got the same email you got last week saying he was fine and in a secluded location doing his navy seal training. As long as we hear something, that's better than not hearing anything at all. He's got his satellite phone and I have mine. Where are you at?"

"I'm still in New York heading back to California in a few. I wanted to check in with you before I left because the next few weeks are going to be hectic,

Even if you don't hear from me, I still expect a text during the week. Remember to stay connected and I'll do my best to do the same. Be careful, bro and I love you."

"I love you too, bro," Cade heard right before Cameron hung up.

He thought about how his life and the lives of his brother's had turned around because of his grandparents and their intervention. It was because of them that he was the actor and business man that he was today.

Back when he first arrived in Chicago to live with them, he was shy and reserved. His brothers were timid and afraid to sleep by themselves. Life for them in Compton had been hard. Life with their grandparents was the complete opposite and when they finally realized they were never going to return to their life in Compton, they began to loosen up.

He tried playing sports, but didn't excel at it. He loved movies and thought that he would make a good actor, so when he saw auditions were needed for a school play for a rugged, thug like character, he jumped at the chance to be a part. He also had a thing for the girl who was going out for the lead female role. At the age of seventeen, he'd gotten that starring role and received kudos for his acting ability. An agent was given a video of the play and sought him out about a role in a movie. Cade's grandparents worked out the deal and a star was born. He wanted to focus on acting full-time, but his grandfather made him promise to get his degree first and that he could take acting gigs while in school.

He went to school at the California Institute of Art that specialized in enhancing his skills as an actor. While in college he expanded his acting ability and with the help of an acting coach, he landed his second major role during his junior year and while he had classes during the day, he starred in a weekly sitcom that filmed at night. The year he graduated he'd taken on the starring role in the biggest action movie of the century and a star was born. With what he knew were good looks he'd gotten from his father, that gig propelled him into the spotlight and the rest, as they say, was history and he never looked back.

He gathered his things, called his team and rushed to make his flight to California. He knew the media would be clamoring around the hotel looking to get shots of him or an interview with him and he wasn't in the mood.

"Aaron, we're leaving from the garage. I don't feel like the media this morning," he said the moment Aaron walked into the suite after he'd sent him a text that he was ready.

"I got you covered. I already worked things out with the hotel. We can use the private exit and we're using your truck from last night with the windows completely tinted. Even if they try and get snapshots of you through the front window, they won't because the divider will be up, so you're good. I take it you're still trying to recover from last night?" Aaron laughed.

Cade laughed along with him.

"I'm still hoping that I do recover because those chicks last night were off the chain. They acted as if they really had something to prove and for a one night stand, they put it all on me and I won't even tell you what they did to me in the shower this morning. All I can say is I'm surprised a brother can stand this morning. What were their names?"

Aaron laughed and shook his head.

"Shameful dude; you are just shameful. With everything I know you did with them, you could at least remember their names."

Cade shook his head and laughed.

"Names? What's that? Who cares what their names are because it's the bodies that speak to me."

"Man, I swear one day you're going to meet a woman who will be immune to your charming ways and just when you least expect it, she's going to turn your world upside down and where you think you're running things, you'll be the follower."

He shook his head in the negative, knowing that would never happen.

"Aaron, how many times have you told me that same thing and how many times do I have to tell you it's never going to happen to your man Cade here. No woman will ever be able to get her hooks that deep into me. All these women want is the fame and fortune that comes along with being on the arm of Cade Weston. They wouldn't know anything deeper if it stared them in the face. It's all surface and I'm okay with that because it's part of the life."

As they headed out, Aaron continued the conversation.

"Don't you ever want anything more than a bunch of nameless faces and sexy bodies? Don't you see yourself having something more than that; something long lasting and meaningful?"

He didn't hesitate with his answer.

"Trust me when I tell you, just because you're all happily married with the best little son anybody could have, and I should know since I'm his godfather, doesn't mean that life is for everyone. You and Misha have a great life and the love that you share is admirable, but that's not in the cards for me. I can't trust that a woman isn't just with me for the fame and fortune. I've chosen this life and how do I really know a woman is being true to me or if she was only being true to my lifestyle."

"You know I love you like a brother. I've been with you since the beginning and I've seen all the women you parade in and out of your bed and when they're gone I also see a man who would love to not have to kick a woman out before you're seen in the light of day with her. Even the big time women like the actresses and models that you've also bedded have no meaning for you. You treat them just like you treat the nameless, limitless number of other women you say goodbye to when the sun comes up in the morning. One day you're going to tire of that and realize there is more to life than money, stardom and sex. Trust me, I have been with you and enjoyed the women along with you, but when Misha came into my life like a thief and stole my heart, I never looked back and it made me see that all the meaningless women I'd gone through didn't compare to what my life is like when I go home and wake up in the morning with her in my arms. The feeling I get when my son wakes up early in the morning and to give her a rest, I get him up and we have fun watching his favorite cartoons and making his favorite breakfast. That's better than any nameless chick or the large amount of money you pay me to keep you safe. I'm just saying, I wouldn't be your friend if I didn't tell you there are some things in life that are better."

Cade listened to every word said and knew his friend spoke from the heart. They'd been friends since back in their college days and when Aaron's career as a football player came to an end with an injury, he brought him on board as head of his security detail and from day one they had been as close as two brothers.

"I hear you Aaron. I love Misha and Aaron, Jr. and I can tell she's been good for you. Our lives are so different and for me the playboy life works. That's all there is for me and I'm good with that.

I've been used enough for leverage by women so much so that I don't think there is an honest one out there for me. Let me have this and I promise I'll start remembering names."

They laughed realizing they needed to lighten the mood.

"I hear you dude and you won't hear me mention it again. You're not working out this morning before you leave?"

"I don't have time to work-out this morning. According to Abby I'm a slacker and I need to get to the airport to catch the flight so I'm not late for my first meeting in Los Angeles later today. Besides, I did get a really good workout all night long last night and early this morning. A brother got all the kinks worked out and it was better than any gym equipment could do. After those two, I needed an oxygen tank just to get up. Am I walking funny?" he asked, parading around the room walking like Red Foxx from the Sanford and Son television show, one of his all-time favorite shows.

Aaron shook his head as he gathered up the luggage and called for his guys to help.

"Yeah, you're walking real funny. I think I see an extra curve in your bowed-legs. It must be a result of the two for one you had last night. Let's go man before you break out in a comedy routine. You're an action star, stay away from comedy."

Cade took one last look around the suite before exiting behind his security detail to head down to the garage. His last thought was that he really had no idea what the names of the two women he'd spent the night with. For the first time in his life, he didn't like that he couldn't remember their names.

4

"Excuse me," Callie said rushing to check in for her flight while almost plowing over a man getting out of a black truck. She didn't bother to turn to see who it was because she was in a hurry. She heard him say it wasn't a problem as she continued on at a fast pace dragging her luggage with her.

When she got inside, she stopped when she saw the long line of people waiting to check in luggage for their flight.

"I will never make my flight," she said to no one in particular.

"Perhaps you should have checked your luggage in at the curbside check-in. That line is always short," she heard a voice behind her say.

She turned around at the sound of the deep, sexy voice and looked up into the face of a very handsome, extremely sexy and downright gorgeous, Cade Weston, the hottest star in Hollywood. He was even better looking in person than he was in magazines and movies. She'd seen every one of his movies and the hotness he exuded on screen didn't compare to the immediate increase in the temperature around her. She knew her reaction to him was something every woman experienced when they saw him whether she was young or old. The man was dazzling and she was sure he knew it.

"Thank you, but since I'm here now I guess I'll just wait. I can't think of dragging this luggage back outside."

Callie turned back around to head in the direction of one of the lines when she felt a light touch on her arm and she turned back around.

"Aaron, get someone to help her with her bags so that she can go back out to the curbside check-in."

Callie was startled at the gesture. It didn't occur to her that someone of his status would care.

"Oh that's not necessary. I don't want to bother anyone," she said.

"Don't worry about it. Men are supposed to help make things easier for any woman in need. I'm Cade and you are?" he asked.

"I know who you are Mr. Weston. There isn't a person alive who doesn't know who you are. My name is Callie Hurston and it's a pleasure to meet you."

"The pleasure is definitely mine when it comes to helping out such a beautiful woman."

One of his men, Sean, from his detail came up and picked up Callie's bags to carry them back out to the curb.

"Tell the attendant outside that Mr. Weston would appreciate it if he could make sure he gets Ms. Hurston checked in on time so that she doesn't miss her flight," Aaron said as Sean walked ahead of Callie.

"Thank you Mr. Weston. I appreciate the help with my luggage," she said.

Callie hoped the look on her face didn't show how intoxicating she thought he was or exactly how enamored she was with him. This was not the time for her body to betray her. Cade Weston had every woman in the world vying for his attention and affection and she need not swoon because he said hello and offered his staff to help her.

"The name is Cade and you're welcome. I'm glad I could help."

Callie nodded and walked away.

As she walked away, Cade watched her every move.

"Damn, that is one beautiful woman. She's more beautiful than any woman I've ever seen. I wonder what her nationality is because her look is exotic and almost mysterious and if you add in that sultry voice, she could make a man lose his mind over her. If she hadn't walked away, I think I would have started foaming at the mouth."

"Stop looking at that woman Cade. You just got out of bed with two women a few hours ago," Aaron said.

He looked at Aaron innocently.

"All I said was that she was beautiful and she is. Come on man, you would have to be blind to not see it."

"I didn't say she wasn't; all I'm saying is don't do it Cade."

"Don't do what?" he said with the look of an innocent child on his face.

"I know that look and I'm telling you don't do it. A blind man can see that she is stunning and she has a body that would put every woman you've ever been linked to, to shame and I'm telling you to let it go. Did you not just spend an exhausting night with two women and you're already on the hunt for the next?" Aaron chuckled while following Cade through to the VIP section of the airport through the crowds of people milling about now that they discovered it was Cade.

As usual, the minute someone spotted him, mass hysteria took place. His security detail along with airport security did their best to get him through the crowd that was beginning to form around him as they walked.

Cameras flashed and people shouted his name as they came up to him asking for an autograph. Cade knew he had time to sign autographs and still make his flight since he had a private jet that wasn't ready yet, so he took the time and made his fans happy. He was happy that the paparazzi were not allowed in this part of the airport or things would be pandemonium.

"I'm thinking of no such thing, but she was fine wasn't she? I mean she was beyond fine. I don't think I've ever seen a woman more naturally beautiful. I know I didn't get to check her out for long, but did you see how gorgeous she was even without a face fully covered in layers of make-up. I won't even talk about the outfit she had on showing she clearly knows how to put an outfit together. It added to her incredible appearance," he said while signing autographs and stopping for photographs with everyone who held up a camera.

"Yeah, I saw all that and like I said, leave it alone and say hello to your fans so we can get you to the VIP section to wait for the jet to take off. You can't sign every autograph request and take every picture."

Before signing his next autograph, he looked in Callie's direction again and caught a glimpse of her through the glass door. What a woman, he thought.

"I'm sorry everyone, but Mr. Weston has a flight he has to catch. We're sorry he won't be able to sign anymore autographs or take anymore pictures. We do have some already signed photographs if anyone would like one of those as well as some free samples of Mr. Weston's new men's cologne in sizes small enough to fit in your carry-on luggage. One of Mr. Weston's assistants will be in the area to your left if you'd like one."

Cade looked up and saw one of his assistants,

David, giving the people who had gathered around him instructions and he was thankful. The crowd was getting larger than they could handle.

"Thanks David," he said, thankful that they always brought David along who was a wiz when it came to handling the fans and providing a distraction with some kind of giveaway to take the focus off of him.

He and the rest of his team moved toward the VIP area to wait on his flight. He entered the secure glassed in area, took a seat and pulled out his IPad to search through what he knew were a ton of emails and texts from Abby that he needed to read since he had a little extra time on his hands.

While he sat and read, he didn't know what caused him to look up, but when he did, his eyes landed once again on the woman he'd helped when he first arrived. He was able to get a good look at her this time and he couldn't seem to take his eyes off of her. He watched her walk up to the ticket counter and noticed that the smile she had as she walked by was now replaced by a frown followed by a heated exchange with the attendant at the counter.

Cade knew that he shouldn't, but he got up anyway and headed in her direction to see what the problem was, noticing that she was clearly distraught. Aaron caught the direction of Cade's stare and stopped him before he opened the door to exit the VIP section.

"What are you doing Cade? You don't have time for this and what is with this superman, save the day guise you've taken on today?" Aaron asked.

"Save it Aaron. I know the story and the plane isn't even ready yet."

Cade ignored any more words from him and walked toward Callie as he listened to her conversation. His detail kept people at bay as he walked up to the counter.

"Wait, how could I have gotten bumped from this flight?" Callie asked the attendant.

"I'm sorry Ms. Hurston. We are using a smaller plane for the flight you were on so the last group of passengers who booked had to be bumped. We are working to get you on a later flight, but that's all I can do at this point, I'm sorry."

"That's not going to help my situation. I need to get to California on that flight or I'm going to be out of a possible job. Are there any other flights going out that I can get on and still get in on time?"

"I'm afraid not because they are all booked. I have a flight leaving in a few hours that I can get you on, but that's the best I can do."

Callie was beyond frustrated hearing she was bumped from a flight one hour before take-off. Before she could say anything else, the attendant had moved on to the next person who was complaining just as she was.

She stood with her mouth gaped open at the way the attendant dismissed her as if she were invisible.

Realizing her pleading was falling on deaf ears, she turned and walked right into the person standing behind her.

"I'm sorry," she said before looking up into the face of Cade Weston again.

"You seem to want to plow me down today Ms. Hurston," he said, smiling.

She was stunned and aroused at the same time seeing him again.

"I apologize that I wasn't paying much attention that time or this one and please call me Callie. Ms. Hurston is my mother," she said.

"Callie it is then. Are you alright because you seem very upset with the attendant."

"It looks like I've been bumped from my flight to Los Angeles and it appears that the attendant doesn't care that I have a job interview that I'll miss if I don't get on my flight as planned. I'm going to try another airline to see what else is available. I hope you aren't hit with a delay like I was because I hear all the flights from this airline are booked."

Cade couldn't stop staring at her, mesmerized by her beauty once again. While she chatted on he took the time to get a better look at her.

Her best feature was her incredibly beautiful face which was blemish free and covered in very light make-up. Her hair was pulled up into a wild, but tamed mass on the top of her head that then cascaded down her back. He could tell from the way it flowed that it was her own long, naturally luxurious mane. She wasn't wearing her outfit, it was wearing her and flattered her in every way from her large breasts to her trim waste which then flared out at her voluptuous hips which were encased in a short but sexy pencil skirt, showing off just how shapely she was.

He couldn't resist the desire to look down at her feet, the part of a woman he considered the sexiest, especially when she maintained them well. When he looked down, he was thrilled to see that hers were perfectly maintained and that they were encased in a pair of high heeled strappy shoes that looked as if they were meant for her feet. He couldn't help when his body hardened at what she would look like if he removed every stitch of her clothing and slid all of that sexiness under him.

He cleared his throat checking back into the conversation. He didn't want her to catch him ogling her.

"Well good luck to you in getting a flight out. Were you headed out to California as well?" she asked trying to hide her nervousness that the world famous actor, Cade Weston, was actually standing and listening to her vent while smiling at her the entire time. Damn he is sexy, she thought and held her lips closed before she said it out loud.

"Actually yes I am, but I'm not going out on this airline. I have a private jet that I'm waiting for and I happened to see that you appeared upset and I was concerned. I'm sorry for eavesdropping on your conversation. I wish there was something I could do to help," he said, meaning every word.

"Oh that's quite alright and I'm fine. You were helpful to me at check-in and if it hadn't been for that I wouldn't have an hour available to try and find another flight. I would still be in the baggage check-in line if you had not leant a helpful hand."

Cade looked up as Aaron appeared in his line of sight behind Callie signaling for him to get moving.

"I had better get to my waiting area to catch my flight. Good luck to you in finding another flight and good luck with the job." He smiled.

"Maybe I was eavesdropping more than I thought."

When she smiled back at him, his body lurched. His desire for her was unmistakable.

Aaron signaled him again and he finally turned and walked away. As he made his way beyond the crowd and into the glass enclosed VIP waiting area he turned again and looked her way, fascinated at the little he knew about her.

"You're doing it aren't you?" Aaron asked as he and others on the team took a seat in the waiting area again.

"I'm not doing anything," he replied, taking his own seat and pulling out his cell to check his texts.

"Are you trying to tell me I didn't just catch you picturing her naked?"

Cade smiled and laughed at the thought.

"Oh, I was way beyond picturing her naked, bro.

Believe me, I already know she'd be one hell of a sight completely naked. It's the completely clothed part that's got my temperature rising. There is something about that woman that I can't shake."

He felt like he was losing it over a woman he'd only met briefly.

"I'm telling you to let it go Cade. You do not have time for a quickie; you have a flight to catch."

Cade looked up at his friend and discounted any idea he may have about his intentions.

"I wasn't even thinking about a quickie dude. I don't think she's the quickie kind of woman. What you see there, my man, is a class act and an incredibly gorgeous one at that."

"Well maybe luck will be on your side and you'll run into her in Los Angeles. I heard her say that's where she was going."

He was hoping for more than luck. Everything in him was telling him he not only wanted, but he needed to see her again. He was afraid to lay that plan on luck being on his side when his plane touched down. Without thinking, he knew what he wanted to do to make sure he hadn't seen the last of her.

"Aaron, I need you to do me a favor."

"I hear you cooking up some scheme and I have an idea I'm not going to like it."

Cade dismissed his reservation.

"Go ask Callie if she'd like to catch a ride on the jet to Los Angeles. I'd hate to see her miss out on that job she was talking to the attendant about. It clearly means a lot to her considering how extremely upset she was about the possibility of not making it there on time."

He watched as Aaron shook his head in the negative, not that he wasn't going to do it, but that he thought it was a bad idea. They had been friends for so long, he knew all of the signals.

"This has bad idea written all over it Cade. You can't have a quickie with that woman on the plane. I know I don't want to hear you thrashing around in the sleeping quarters and I didn't bring my noise-cancelling earphones."

Cade laughed out loud.

"Aaron, will you give it a rest already? Give me a little more credit than that. I promise you I am not trying to have any kind of quickie with her. I only want to offer her a ride to Los Angeles because I have the room and she needs a ride. Clearly she's following a dream and if no one knows what that means, I do. She may even say no, but I want to at least make the offer."

Aaron didn't say anything else as he stood to leave the VIP area to walk in the direction that they'd seen Callie go in. Before he exited through the glass door, he turned back to Cade.

"Do you realize, you've said her name more than once? You never remember names, but hers flows out of your mouth as if it takes very little effort to remember it."

He didn't realize he'd done that, but Aaron was right. He was horrible at remembering names, but he remembered hers and in his mind he was saying it over and over again. She was that unforgettable.

"Everything about that woman is unforgettable, let alone her name and if you stand here chatting with me any longer, I may miss my chance to play hero to a damsel in distress."

He watched as Aaron and Sean went in search of Callie and he waited patiently hoping to get the chance to sit across from her on the flight to Los Angeles where he hoped to learn more about her. Something about her was intriguing and he wanted to find out why.

5

Everyone on the flight was finally settled into their seats and Cade smiled like a kid in a candy story as he looked across at Callie who had taken the seat directly across from him. He was glad his plan had seats that faced each other.

"Thank you for the offer of the ride on your jet," she said. "I was hesitant at first because I really didn't want to seem like I couldn't figure out my own problem."

As feisty as he knew she was, he had no doubt she would have worked it out. The problem was they may not have ended up across from each other if she had.

"I didn't think that at all. We were both going to the same place and I had the room. So tell me about this job you're going out to Los Angeles for."

It was a long flight and Callie saw no harm in

being nice since he was being nice to her.

"Well, I'm a stylist and I have the opportunity to work on this new series that's going to start in a few months."

"Wait, I know I've heard your name before. Weren't you the main stylist to the stars for that hit reality show that films in New York City?"

Hearing him mention the show made her skin crawl and her pulse quickened. Being the big star that he is, she should have known that he would have heard about all of the drama surrounding her release from the show as the main stylist. Things like that travel around fast. She didn't want to carry-on with the conversation afraid of where it would lead, but she didn't want to be rude either.

"Yes, that was me. I'm not working on that anymore and I'm hoping for my next level up with this job."

"Being a stylist fits you well as I can tell from your own attire. You look very nice, by the way."

She blushed.

"Thank you."

"How long have you been in this line of work?" he asked.

"About five years now. I've been blessed to have walked out of college and have had some very lucrative contracts styling some famous people."

"I know how it feels to be walking in what you were meant to do. I feel the same way about my life. Since we have a long flight, would I be intruding if I asked you to tell me more about you? Where are you from and do you have family on the west coast?"

"Not at all."

She crossed her legs and settled back into the plush, butter yellow leather seats.

"I'm originally from Texas where my parents still live. My dad owns one of the top real estate firms in Dallas and my mom works with him. I have an older sister who owns several very successful beauty bars in Dallas. I don't think I have any family on the west coast, but who knows. This trip was sort of a last minute opportunity and I didn't check with my parents to see if there was any family out here I could drop in on and say hello to. What about you? I know what the internet, magazines and papers say about you, but what else is there about you that they don't say?"

Cade sat back, crossed his legs and relaxed as he began sharing his life as she had done with him. He knew he had to cross his legs because watching her cross hers and checking out the sexy curve to her legs had his body reacting in an embarrassing way if she'd noticed. He willed his body to calm down as he talked.

"Well most of what they print about where I came from is pretty much on point. What it doesn't say is that I was born and raised in Compton until my father died and my mother disappeared. My grandparents came to get me and my two brothers and raised us. I was about fourteen back then. I have two younger brothers, one is in college in Florida and the other is in the military."

Callie listened while he talked and couldn't believe how comfortable she felt being around him. While his team slept quietly, the two of them continued to talk for the rest of the flight. She couldn't help but give him the once over while they were sitting in close proximity to each other. Television, movie theater screens and magazines did not do him justice. He was fine and she could see why women went crazy anytime he was around.

Looking at him she could tell he was African American, with some other type of heritage mixed in which added to his salient good looks. She'd been around people up close and personal for years and she could tell he was probably African American and Puerto Rican or Hispanic. His skin color was a chestnut brown and though his hair was close-cut, it had a dark, straightened appearance that didn't come from chemicals, but heritage. His facial features reminded her of a herculean look which was strong, stout and chiseled. The man was flawless. What she hadn't noticed in many magazine pictures was his eye color.

From pictures she'd seen of him, she thought his eyes were a lightened shade of brown, but they were in fact hazel which added to his mystique appearance. He was captivating and irresistibly so.

Even though he was seated, she knew the talk of

the town about Cade Weston was his legs. He had the sexiest walk on a pair of bowed legs that seemed to go on for miles and everyone who commented about him mentioned that first. The man could wear a pair of jeans and she knew from his clothing line that each pair he wore were specifically made just for him.

He had a self-awareness about him that spoke not of cockiness, but of confidence which she was sure was what carried him as far as it had in his career. He was a known to be a risk taker who stood up to challenges and to her, those were two character traits she thought made men their sexiest.

"So, I hear you could be getting a nod later this year from the Academy for your last film. I saw it and loved it and I see by the almost one billion dollar take so far that it's slated to land in the same group with some of the best movies of all times. That's not even counting the revenue that will come in from the video sales once it's eventually released. That's quite an achievement for someone your age."

She knew from reading stories about him that he was thirty-one and one of the youngest men to ever acquire the type of wealth in the entertainment industry at his age.

"It certainly has been a wild ride and if I get the nod, I'll be thankful for it. If not, I'm still glad that I was a part of a movie that had a world-wide impact. I'm already reading over the script for my next movie and we should begin shooting in a few months. While I have this break until then, I have a few business ventures I'm working on including executive producing a new television show. Season one is about to start and we're about to begin filming season two soon."

Callie found him fascinating and it appears there is a lot more to him than what the media portrays. She knew he was a great actor, a great businessman and of course a playboy, but she was glad to hear he was expanding his craft, taking Hollywood by the horns.

"Is this something you can tell me about? I promise I won't leak anything to the media," she quipped getting a smile and a hearty laugh out of him.

"It's not a secret that the show is coming out, but it is a secret that I'm executive producing it with a friend. We recently formed a production company together and this will be our first project. I'm hoping attaching my name to it will give it a running start. Critics can be characteristically brutal, but I'm thinking my fan base will shut them up if they don't like it and be forced to give it a serious look at. It's a positive drama series with the main characters being four guys with careers that end up connecting them together and through the friendship that grows they solve mysteries. A lot of the details for season two are still being worked out, but I think with the storylines that the writing team have come up with, it will be a hit. We need more positive shows on television. These reality shows that aren't really reality shows are tearing our peoples' heritage to shreds and I'm hoping to bring better shows to television through this new partnership."

"That's truly admirable and I agree. I can hardly stand to turn the television on these days. I'm looking forward to checking out this new show."

They talked for the next couple of hours until the pilot said they would soon be landing. As they talked, Cade learned even more about his guest.

He found out that her best friend was getting married and had asked her to design the dresses. He also listened while she shared with him her dreams of having her own clothing line. He admired the drive in her to go after her dreams and not let anything stand in her way. He liked that he didn't get the groupie vibe from her which is what he could usually read as soon as he met a woman.

"So tell me more about your dream of having your own clothing line one day. Just how good are your designs?" he smiled.

"I wouldn't be me if I didn't say that I think they're fantastic. If I don't think so then no one else will either," she exclaimed while smiling back.

"Well if you're like any other designer I know, you're packing some shots or sketches in one of those bags of yours. Are they are secret or can I get a look at anything. I promise I won't steal any ideas since you know I have my own lines of clothing as well. I really want to see your vision. Do you mind showing me?" he asked.

"Not at all," she said reaching into her bag for her sketch pad and handing it to him.

"These are some of the one's I've already made and patented. I made sure no one was going to steal my original designs."

"That's smart thinking on your part," he said, admiring her even more. The more he talked to her, the more he liked and respected her drive and intelligence. She had her head on straight and in the game.

He flipped through several pages and had to admit she definitely had great talent.

"These are incredible and I can see why you want to get these out. They're going to be a big hit. What's holding you back right now if I'm not intruding?" he asked.

"Nothing is holding me back other than myself. I have to get to a place in my life where I have everything in place that I need and then I'll expand my goal even more. I believe that everything happens when it's meant to. I'll get there without a doubt."

"Do you have a website that features the styles of those you've worked with? I want to see what your taste is like."

Callie reached her hand out in a gesture for him to hand her his electronic device.

"I'll pull it up for you. Everyone I've ever styled

is featured on my website. Having that allows people all over the world to see what I can do. I'm very proud of my work."

She quickly typed in her website and handed it back to him.

"These are hot!" he expressed going from screen to screen.

"Thank you."

"I love your style and it brings out a lot of the personality in the person. I know all of these people and I can see that the clothes fit who they really are and I like that. You are very talented Callie and I expect your career will take you very far. I wish you all the success in the world."

As they landed and waited to be told they could exit the plane, Callie turned on her cell-phone and noticed she had several voicemail messages. She checked them and stopped in her tracks after listening to the first message. She tried not to let disappointment show as she gathered her things to leave the plane.

Cade could tell something had changed in her by her body language. After listening to her voicemail messages, she seemed upset, but tried to hide it. Since they would be exiting the airport in a private area, he asked his team to go ahead while he stayed back with her while she gathered her belongings.

"Are you going to continue to act like something isn't wrong? What is it? I can tell the difference in you since you checked your messages."

She didn't want to say. She revealed more to this man about herself than she'd told anyone in years and he'd already helped her as if she were a lost cause and she didn't want him to think she was trying to get anything out of him.

"It was nothing; I'm fine," she lied without looking at him.

"Try again Callie. What happened?" he asked, really concerned.

She hesitated before telling him, not wanting to lie.

"They already hired someone for the job I was supposed to be interviewing for. Apparently they'd left several messages for me, but I forgot I turned my cell phone off when I got in the cab back in New York. I meant to turn it back on and forgot when it seemed like I kept running into one problem after another. They knew I was coming in from New York and tried to catch me before I left."

"I'm sorry to hear that and you've already come all this way. If you want I can probably get the jet to take you back home if you like. I'm not using it for a few weeks."

"Oh I couldn't ask that. You've done so much for me already and you didn't have to considering you didn't even know me. If nothing else, I still have the hotel for five days and I still have another job that I'll be doing so the trip is not a total loss. The last message said since they were unable to reach me and thinking that I was probably already on my way, they would still cover my hotel for the days I was scheduled to be here. I'm going to stay and see if I can get any other leads on other opportunities. The other job is scheduled to start in a few weeks if I didn't take this one so I could use the down time and I can't think of a better way to do that than to spend a few days in California. The company that I was interviewing with was covering the five days of the hotel and I was covering the next five of my ten day stay here since my best friend was coming out. I still want to hang with her so I'm going to stay. Thank you for your hospitality Cade. It was unexpected yet appreciated."

Cade really liked her and got more enjoyment out of the few hours they'd talked than he had out of conversations with all of the women he'd known.

"Well I'm glad I could help. I'll tell you what, I hate the thought that you may be stranded if you want to return home before your scheduled time. Am I asking too much if we can exchange numbers? You can call me if you find you do want to go back early and like I said, I'm not using my jet for the next several weeks and I can have Carlos, my pilot take you back and then return here when it's time for me to head to Chicago to visit my grandparents before I start shooting my movie."

Who was this man? Callie thought. He was nothing like she thought he would be. She assumed he would be arrogant like many big, handsome stars or that he would try and get under her skirt which he had not tried to do.

"Exchanging numbers is okay with me," she said.

Cade read off his number to her and told her to dial his number so that he could lock it into his cell phone. Afterward, he helped her with her carryon bags and they exited the plane.

"It was a pleasure meeting you Callie. Talking to you was a breath of fresh air. I wish you every bit of luck in your career and who knows, perhaps we'll run into each other again soon. We're in the entertainment business and I have no doubt, we will soon cross paths."

"Thank you Cade. You have been a knight in shining armor and I appreciate it. Good luck with the Academy nod and with the new movie and show. I would congratulate you on everything you shared with me that you have going on, but then we'd never get out of here," she laughed and so did he.

"Thank you and be safe," he said as he ventured in one direction after making sure she knew where to get her luggage that's being held in the VIP area. Before he lost sight of her, he smiled when she turned and waved before turning around a corner out of his view.

What an incredible woman, he said out loud as he walked in the direction of his team.

"I see you found your way to us," Aaron said, leaning again his truck in a private area of the airport garage.

"I had to be sure she was on her way before I left. I did bring her to California on my jet," he said.

"I'm sure that was the only reason," Aaron said snidely.

He knew why Aaron said it, but it still disturbed him and he wasn't sure why.

"Don't read too much into it. I was just helping her out and that's it. Save the strange look on your face for another time. There's nothing there, man."

Cade could still see the accusatory look on his face as he took his seat in the back of the truck. He was about to shut the door when Aaron leaned in.

"Tell me this and I'll leave it alone."

Cade didn't look at him, but instead looked down at his phone reading texts and emails.

"Did you get her number?"

Hearing that, he did look up and before he could respond, Aaron stopped him with a hand.

"No need to respond because I can tell by the silly look on your face that you did. Just remember what I said back in New York about that one woman who would turn your world upside down; I think you just met her."

On that Aaron shut the door and got in the front passenger seat of the truck.

Aaron was off for the next few days and was glad to be back in Los Angeles to spend quality time with his wife and son before he had to be back on duty with Cade in a few days. He had a feeling when he returned to work, things were going to take a drastic turn in Cade's private life. He may not see it, but Aaron did. His boss and friend had the same look on his face that he had the minute he'd met his wife Misha. It was the look of a man who was snagged hook, line and sinker. He smiled knowing it wouldn't be a bad thing if he could convince his friend to be open to it. They were like brothers and he wanted more for his friend than more money than he could spend and the countless number of nameless bed partners that didn't fill the need for a woman who could love him unconditionally like he'd found in his wife.

He noticed that Cade never said another word as they pulled up to the location where the press conference was taking place. He would have about an hour to get dressed and ready.

He made sure Cade was secure inside of the five star hotel before turning over the security detail to the next shift of guys. After giving them instructions on all of the things Cade had going on for the next few days, he got back into the truck, smiled again knowing Cade had no idea what was in store for him and had the driver pull off. Callie Hurston was about to become a big part of their lives.

6

"Finally, you're here," Abby said as Cade rushed into the room where the press conference was about to begin with the announcement of Cade's new athletic foot wear line and the announcement that the number one basketball draft pick would be endorsing it.

He smiled knowing the spitfire he hired as his assistant would dig into him the moment he showed up and she never failed.

"I told you I would be here Abby and I am. I've been here for over an hour in my room changing. Can we have one day where you tone it back a little and cut me some slack?"

"Not on your life. You didn't hire me to be toned down; you hired me because I'm a ball buster and that's what I'm going to be. You've been singing this same song for ten years and by now you should know that I'm not going to change. If it weren't for me, your life would be a mess. You're late and I've done everything except tricks in order to drag this out while we waited on you, so get in there and let's get this press conference going. What took you so long anyway? I know when you arrived and I know it didn't take you an hour to change into this suit and tie," she said fussing over him by straightening his already straightened tie and smoothing down the sleeves of the suit jacket that he knew had no wrinkles.

"I had a few phone calls to make and it doesn't matter because I'm here now. Where do you want me?"

"I'm glad you followed my advice and left the jeans home. I know jeans are your signature look and people are accustomed to seeing you in them, but this is a great opportunity to showcase the newest line of suits by *Cado*. You are sitting in the vacant seat on the left of our star player. Everything is ready to go and I'm hoping you looked over the questions I know you'll be asked."

"Of course I did," he lied. "That's another reason I was late. I don't know what I'd do without you," he said. He had to admit that hiring her was the best decision he'd ever made.

"Yeah, you probably say that to all the women who are helping you build this empire. It's show time."

Cade took the stage and the camera flashes went wild. After two hours of answering questions and taking more photos than he could ever remember taking at one time, he left the stage and had a few hours before he had to get to his next meeting about the new television series he was executive producing.

"I need to get some grub before I'm shuttered off to the meeting about the show. Abby, let's get lunch and go over my schedule for the next two months. I want to carve out some time to go home to Chicago and I also want to go over the list of scripts I've been getting for movies. After we wrap up shooting for my next movie, I want some time to get out and promote *Cado*. Since I'm also the model for my line of clothing, I need to make the necessary rounds to keep people talking about it. That last photo shoot helped double our sales."

"I still say it was the shirtless photos that did the trick. Do you want to do lunch in a private room here at the hotel? If not, we won't get much work done with fans and the media following your every move."

"No, you know what I want. Ask Mitchell can we use his office in the back of the restaurant."

Abby grabbed her phone to make the call to Cade's favorite restaurant. He and Mitchell had become good friends over the years and Cade's presence and kudos about the food at the restaurant turned the spot into one of the hottest in Los Angeles.

"You're set," she said.

"Good because I'm starving. While we're on our

way, tell me what else is on my schedule for today."

Abby looked at Cade like she didn't know who he was.

"What?"

"Nothing, except for the fact that you're a lot more chipper than you usually are, especially when you have a day of press events and meetings. What gives?"

"I'm just having a good day. Let's go before my mood changes."

Cade didn't want to say that his thoughts kept drifting to Callie and he hoped she was settled in at her hotel. His cell phone buzzed and his smiled brightened even more when he noticed a text from her making sure he had her number and she also thanked him for being nice to her when she knew he didn't have to be. He quickly typed back a response letting her know he was happy that he could help and that he enjoyed her company. He was still smiling like a Cheshire cat when Abby stopped talking.

"Are you even listening to me Cade?"

He heard nothing because he was too focused on the text message on his phone. He didn't tell anyone, but he hadn't stopped thinking about her since he'd left her at the airport. He couldn't place his finger on it, but there was something about Callie that stuck with him and seeing the text message from her letting him know she had arrived safely at her destination made him smile and he'd been caught by the last person he wanted in her personal business. He continued typing, ignoring her and trying to remember to not smile.

"Cade, stop ignoring me. I know you hear me. You know how I can pester until you respond to me so you may as well tell me what's going on."

"Nothing is going on Abby. I'm merely returning a text which is something you do when someone texts you," he jibed.

"Right and that stupid grin on your face is something that you usually do as well when you're texting someone back. What gives?"

He looked up and saw the stern look on her face and knew he wasn't going to get away with changing the subject; at least not this time.

"It's nothing Abby. I gave someone a ride on the jet from New York and she was texting me to say thanks."

"She?"

"Yes Abby, I said she. There's nothing there so move on."

"Uh, oh, I hear a story coming out of this. I don't even know if I want the details. Just tell me you didn't get naked thirty-thousand feet in the air."

"You got jokes I see. I won't even attempt to address that considering this woman is a classy lady and I also don't know her that well. All I did was offer her a ride so that she wouldn't miss an appointment and that's it."

"Is that the only ride you offered her? You know

how you are with that free-spirited zipper of yours that doesn't know how to stay up around a woman."

"Can we get me some food and drop this ridiculous conversation about my personal life, something you know we're not about to stand here and discuss."

Abby dropped the subject sensing that there was something different about how Cade was talking about this woman. She wasn't sure she'd ever heard him mention woman and classy in the same sentence before.

**

After a lunch that had him feeling like he needed to take forty winks, Cade walked into the meeting room where everyone was already buzzing with millions of ideas of how the second season should go since they pretty much had season one wrapped up.

"Okay team, let's get to business. What's up first?" he asked, picking up the piles of papers in front of him and perusing them.

"Well for starters, we still have our head stylist to hire," one of the team members at the table said.

As soon as he heard the word stylist, he didn't hear much else. His thoughts turned to Callie and knew she would be perfect for the position. If his team liked her, he'd get the chance to talk to and see her again.

"The top sheet is the list of stylists that were recommended to us based on their history of working on shows similar to ours. I know we talked about a new stylist for season two so let's narrow the list down and select one," another person at the table said.

Cade picked up the list and checked it out before interrupting with an idea of his own.

"Listen, I have someone I want you to add to the top of the list."

"Cade, we already have a long list to go through and all of these people are already scheduled this week for interviews. Are you sure you want to add new names at this late date?" one of the head writers asked.

Cade looked over at him as if to ask why he was being questioned.

"I'm sure, so make room for one more person on your list. I'll text her number to Abby to do the reach out to her. Her name is Callie Hurston, she's out of New York and I want her name at the top of the list. She's here in Los Angeles for the next week or so and I'm sure once you see what she has to bring to the table, you'll be as interested as I am."

"No problem boss. You've seen her work and you're impressed?" another team member asked.

"I've seen some of her sketches and I've also checked out her website. She's styled some big time artists over the past few years and I think she'd bring a lot to the image we're looking for. She should be contacted and brought up to date on what we're looking for so that she can have some time to get her ideas together. She hasn't had the time that all of the other potentials have had and if her schedule permits, schedule her interview last and let's see if she'd be a good fit."

Cade knew no one would question what he wanted as they continued on with the meeting.

"I'll send her a quick text to let her know to expect a call from someone today?" he asked looking around the table with his gaze and question landing on a quizzical looking Abby.

"She'll be contacted as soon as this meeting is over," Abby replied.

Cade grabbed his phone and shot Callie a quick text and went on with his meeting.

**

Callie was about to call Angel to let her know she was in Los Angeles and to find out what time her flight was getting in when it buzzed signaling a text message. Cade's name popped up and she smiled a silly school girl grin.

"Stop it girl. This man is not interested in you and even if he was, you know how bad getting involved with any celebrity could turn out," she said to herself and checked the message.

She sat straight up when she saw that his text was giving her the heads up that she would be getting a call from someone on his team about a job as a stylist on the television show he'd mentioned on the flight.

"What!" she screamed before grasping how loud

she'd shouted. She covered her mouth before a second scream exited.

She thought of what she should say back and didn't want to seem too needy or overzealous. She had been thinking about reaching out to some contacts while she had the extra time and never thought in a million years that Cade would reach out with a job offer.

Her happiness dimmed when she thought of the possibility that his offer could possibly come with some strings attached. He had a proclivity for bedding just about every women he was spotted with and she knew the look of an interested man.

He couldn't hide his interest in her because she saw that look from men all the time. She hadn't seen it from someone as famous as he was, but it was the same look. She thought about saying thanks, but no thanks to his offer, but she didn't want to turn away what could be a great opportunity for her. It was up to her to keep everything professional as she knew that she could.

She thought through her response and replied back that she appreciated it and looked forward to the phone call. She waited while he replied back, "cool" and she threw her phone on the bed and danced around. She knew this wasn't an offer for a job, but a chance to show if she had what it took and she was ready for the challenge.

Forcing any negative thoughts about any strings being attached to the back of her mind, she reached for her phone to call Angel.

"Angel, girl when does your flight get in?" she asked the minute Angel answered.

"I'm just getting to the airport and my flight takes off in about two hours. I can't wait to see you. How was your flight?"

She was about to tell her about Cade and all that happened, but decided to wait until she was at the hotel. If she mentioned it now, Angel would want to hear all of the details and she wanted to tell her over drinks. They had a lot of catching up to do.

"I'll tell you all about it when you get here."

"What time is the interview today? I can't wait to hear about it when I get there."

Callie didn't want to talk about the interview that wasn't going to happen.

"Girl, we can talk about all the work you want to talk about when you get here. I wanted to be sure you were still coming. You'll only be here for a few days and we have a lot to talk about."

"Well, I'm glad to hear you're chipper. I know you have been down lately about what happened in New York and I figured I'd be coming to Cali to cheer you up, but it looks like you don't need cheering up."

"I'm all good Angel. You know nothing can really keep me down. I've encountered mess like what happened with Asia and Mateo before and I'm not sweating it. There will be other opportunities and we'll talk more about that when you get here too.

I'm picking up my rental car in a bit and I'll be waiting at the airport when you get in."

"I hope you have some good fun lined up because I need it. Let's go out and find some men!"

"Girl, stop it. You are engaged to be married and I won't be party to you messing that up by letting you get caught up in this Cali life."

"Girl, I'm not talking about for me, I'm talking about for you. Don't you think it's time to get the dust off and get you some? How long has it been now? The girls and I are going to have to vote you off the island soon. You're giving being single and sexy a bad name."

"Angel, I am not looking for a man or a relationship. I'm too focused on my career and I don't have time for the mess that comes along with men these days."

"So you've had a few rotten apples, don't let it turn you off of men totally, not that you're changing sides or anything. I'm saying, don't let what has happened to you in the past impact your ability to find mister right or even mister right now. I know you have it poppin' in the business world, but it's time to get your personal life in order and have some fun. It doesn't have to be anything serious. I'm talking about enjoying your time in California with all of those fine men. I have no doubt the vultures have already been circling as they often do with you. I'm coming to Cali to help you let your hair down, throw caution to the wind and get loose.

You're too uptight and you need to unwind, but we'll talk about that too when I get there. I'll call you when I land."

Callie hung up and flopped back on the bed. Talking to Angel reminded her that she was man-less. Men were a subject she didn't want to broach and had no intentions of going over her history when Angel came to town. She hasn't had the best of luck in the man department and she would prefer to focus on her career.

She'd had a few relationships and all had turned out bad because she had expectations of more than just a physical relationship and each time she'd been wrong about the intentions of the men she'd been involved with. She hoped, like most women did, that she would find a satisfying relationship and she knew one day she would. For now, that wasn't her focus.

An image of Cade Weston entered her mind and she quickly dismissed it. It was men like him that she always seemed to be drawn to. He was the typical playboy type and she had no doubt he had women in all fifty states. There wasn't a woman alive that didn't find him irresistible and for her own sake, she needed to resist his good looks and charm.

7

"Hey Callie, it's Cade. I want to congratulate you on getting the job as one of the stylists on the show. I was also wondering if I could steal you away to have a celebratory drink to celebrate. I figured I could also give you some insight into my vision for the styles I have in mind for the cast."

She was stunned that Cade had actually called her himself and then that feeling turned to apprehension when he asked her out for what sounded like a date under the guise of talking about work. She appreciated that he was responsible for giving her the opportunity, but she needed to be very clear where the line was drawn without ruining her chance to work on the show.

"I appreciate that you referred me to your staff for the position. I think the show is going to be a huge hit and I'm excited about working on it."

She paused before continuing hoping that she hadn't said the wrong thing.

Cade noticed the pause as well.

"I sense you're hesitating and I feel like there's something you want to say, but aren't saying."

"I'm not sure meeting for a drink is a good idea. I want to be sure this is all about business and nothing else."

"Listen, I would be lying if I said I didn't find you attractive or that I didn't want to know more about you, but I want you to know that you got this job because my team thought you were exactly what was needed. I did refer you to them, but you getting the job was all you; I had nothing to do with the vote. I'd definitely like the opportunity to see you again before production starts. I don't see what harm it could do and besides, are you telling me you wouldn't want to have a drink with me?" he insinuated.

This must be the heartthrob everyone talks about, she thought. His tone suggested he assumed because he was making a play for her, she should jump at the chance because of who he is, which is every woman's dream. She's had her experiences with men like him and from lessons learned, she was now paying attention to all the warning signs.

"Does that really work?" she asked boldly.

"Does what really work?"

"You show interest in a woman and she goes along with the plan like a snake to a charmer."

He wanted to feel insulted, but she spoke the truth. If he asked, women typically came running without question. He'd never encountered one who turned him down and then questioned his motives.

"I didn't ask you to drop your clothes and lay down Callie. I merely asked if you'd like to have a drink with me to celebrate the job offer."

"Do you often ask women you work around out for celebratory drinks and it not end up in a bed someplace?"

She was a tough one and he loved it. Tough, beautiful, sexy and feisty!

He didn't answer, but instead avoided the question all together not wanting to admit that in his past he had coerced a few women who worked around him into bed. It would make him sound like a womanizer and he wanted her to see him in a positive light.

"Well am I at least allowed to send you a bottle of wine to welcome you to the team?"

She smiled when he appeared to back off from sharing a drink together. She saw no harm in the gift.

"Yes. That you can do and thank you. Your assistant has my address and again I appreciate the referral. I guess I'll see you at the next production meeting," she said.

"Are you sure I can't convince you to have a quick drink with me? I swear I'm harmless?"

Callie laughed after getting a feeling that he

wasn't the type to give up.

"I doubt if I would call having a drink with you harmless. I'm going to have to pass on the drink."

Cade was defeated, but he never gives up. He smiled knowing he would try another time since he knew where she'd be working.

After ending the call, he put his cell phone away and turned around coming face to face with Aaron who stood with a shocked look on his face.

"Don't tell me Cade Weston got turned down by a woman? This has to be a first for you brother."

Cade shook it off even though he was right.

"Can you believe that? She actually turned down my invitation to go out for a drink. Me!" he said not believing it himself.

"The usual charm and appeal didn't work. Wait, maybe you needed to ask in person. I mean, no one can turn down the Cade Weston charm in person after you charm and blink those hazel eyes that drives them crazy. I bet that will do it," Aaron jibed.

"Normally I ask for more and I get it, but in this case, all I asked for was a drink. I could have poured on the charm, but usually it doesn't take all that because after all, I am Cade Weston."

"You need to get off of yourself brother. Apparently the fact that you're Cade Weston doesn't mean as much to her as it means to you. I don't think you're going to bag this one."

"I like her and not only because she's gorgeous. Any man would be crazy to not ask her out. I'm serious when I say I really like her."

"I could have told you that and now that she's proven that she's not the typical woman looking to be seen with you or bedded by you because you asked, I think you'll have your work cut out for you. I'm assuming this entanglement with her is not over with?"

"Oh, it's just beginning my brother. Who would have thought that there was a woman who was immune to my charming personality and dashing good looks? I do believe this is the first time I've ever encountered this and you know what? I'm going to take a step back and approach this a different way. I see that what usually works won't work and what I usually want is not what's on my agenda. Of course, I'm still interested in getting up close and personal with her, but I think for the first time, I want to make it more than that. She bewilders me and from that plane ride from New York to California, I know that she's someone I not only want to know more about, but I need to know more about."

Aaron shook his head knowing their lives were about to get very interesting.

"Let's get you out of here. You have several appointments today and there's already a crowd gathering outside waiting for you to exit. Do you want to avoid them and have the car brought around to the rear entrance?"

Cade enjoyed avoiding the media when he could,

but today he felt like being in the midst of all the action.

"Let's go out the front. I need the boost to my ego after Callie turned me down. I'll answer a few questions and let them get a few snapshots. I can't always avoid them if I'm going to stay on top!"

Four days later

Callie was enjoying her first day meeting with the production team for the television show. Angel was spending her last day in California at the spa while she tended to some business. The meeting about the designs for the main characters was just wrapping up when Cade entered the room and all attention turned to him as he took a seat around the table. She tried not to look his way, but it was hard to do because his presence demanded so much attention.

She hadn't had any communication with him after she gave him a call thanking him for the flowers and the bottle of wine he'd sent her congratulating her on joining the team.

When she looked his way, he smiled before asking how the meeting was going. Everyone gave their opinion and shared some of the decisions on the styles for the cast. She pushed thoughts of him from her mind and focused on the discussion.

Cade was pleased to see that Callie was fitting in with the team. Several people shared how some of the ideas for change in the lead characters' style was Callie's idea; ideas that were an improvement over what the team had originally planned.

"I'm glad to hear everything is going well. We're set to begin production soon and I want everything ready. Our audience will be watching each episode and I want them turning in each week, not only for the good story lines, but also because they want to see what the characters will have on next. The visual is just as important as the catchy plots," he added.

Callie watched as others stood to leave and she began gathering her things to do the same. Before she reached the door, Cade asked to speak to her before she left. When every eye in the room turned to her, she felt an uneasiness. She held her head up and smiled as she turned back to Cade who was still sitting at the table.

When the room was clear, Cade turned so that he was giving her his full attention.

"I wanted to ask you what you thought about being on the team. I know it's been a fast-paced whirlwind for you and I want to be sure everything is going well."

"Everything is going great and everyone's being helpful."

"Good to hear. I know you were planning to return to New York before. Have you made plans to extend your stay here?"

"Yes. I'm going to stay at the hotel since they

have long-term accommodations and I really like it. It's not far from the set and I don't have to pack up or look for another place. I'm going to go home for a few days in a couple of days to grab some extra things and then return to focus on my growing list of tasks."

"Did your friend ever make it here?"

"Yes. Angel's been having a blast the past few days. She'll be heading back to Texas tomorrow."

"I'm glad she's having a good time. Listen I'm having a party at my hotel later tonight and I wanted to invite you and Angel. It's nothing too big, but it'll be fun and I'm sure you'd like a moment to relax and get away from work for an evening. I understand you all have had some pretty late nights the past two nights here on the set."

"Thanks Cade, but Angel and I are planning to chill her last night here. There are a lot of details about her wedding we want to go over and who knows when I'll see her again. I hope your party turns out great. I've heard about your parties and I'm sure it will be a who's who in the entertainment world."

"Don't believe all those stories and this one is actually not about the Hollywood scene, but more of just a bunch of close friends. Maybe when you have some down time after you get back from New York, you would consider joining me for lunch one day. I'd like to hear more about your dream of having your own line one day. Maybe it's something

I can help you with."

She didn't like what he was insinuating, as if she would be the kind of woman to take advantage of his fame and fortune in order to get ahead. Clearly he was still trying to get her to agree to go out with him, something she had no interest in doing.

"I don't think that will be a good idea. I want to keep things strictly professional and though I appreciate your offer about my clothing line, I want to do it when the time is right for me and I can do it on my own. I hope you can understand that."

Cade tried not to show his disappointment.

"Sure I understand that. So you won't have a drink with me, you won't go to lunch with me and you turned down the invitation to my party. Do I have a disease that I don't know about or am I butt ugly to you? What's the deal?"

She didn't want the conversation to turn ugly so she held her composure and spoke from her heart.

"I think you're a nice guy and we both know butt ugly is not a term anyone would use to describe you. I want to keep everything about business and that's it."

"Are you seeing anyone right now?" he inquired.

"No I'm not seeing anyone at the moment. I'm focusing on my career which takes up all of my time. It's nothing personal; it's really about what I want to focus on right now and what I don't want is any distractions that could hurt my credibility as a serious stylist."

"I'll tell you what I will do; I will stop hounding you about going out since it's clear you are focused and I don't want to be a distraction. My offer still stands about the party and I'll leave your name and a guest for entrance to the party if you decide to change your mind. It won't be a date because there'll be a lot of people there including some from the production staff. It'll give you an opportunity to mingle in with them before everyone has to put on their all work and no play hats."

"I appreciate the offer, but as I stated, Angel and I are going to relax at my hotel tonight especially since she has an early flight tomorrow morning. Have a great time at your party," she said before turning toward the door.

She looked back one last time before she opened the door and left. She saw a confused look on his face and assumed it was because not many people said no to him. She said no and she planned to continue to do so in order to avoid getting caught up in the personal life of Cade Weston. She had a feeling it would not turn out well for her.

That thought stayed on her mind as she made her way through traffic. When she'd first encountered him at the airport she was just as intrigued as everyone else who meets Cade. He'd helped her more times in a short period of time than any person had in years that wasn't a family member. Was she being difficult in turning down everything he asked? Was there really harm in sharing a drink or lunch with him? The thought of doing both made her remember the drama of her past with other men and knew she'd done the right thing.

She tried to shake off thoughts of Cade and called Angel to see if she needed to pick up anything extra while making her way back to the hotel.

"Hey Angel. I'm on my way back and I wanted to see if I should bring anything back. I don't know if I want hotel food tonight and I definitely don't want to go out. What are you in the mood for food wise?"

"I don't know. Anything works for me. How did you meeting go? Did Cade show up?"

Callie chuckled. "You are such a groupie, Angel!"

"Girl, please. There isn't a woman in this world who is not a groupie for Cade Weston, except for you and for the life of me I can't figure out why. So did he show up or what?"

"Yeah, he showed up and asked me out again and this time it was for lunch and before you ask, yes I turned him down again. I'm not going out with that man. You know my track record and I can't afford a repeat of my past mistakes. I'm keeping my distance and you know how much the media follows his every move. No way am I setting myself up for that. Oh, he also invited us to a party he's having tonight, but I decline that invitation as well."

"You mean you're not going to the party after he

gave you a personal invitation and he invited you to bring me along? You know me girl, you did not meet me yesterday. I want to go!"

"We still have a lot to do and I don't want to spend your last night here in a room full of people. I promise the next time there's a big party, I'll fly you out and we'll go. I'm not ready to rub elbows yet."

Angel relented.

"Alright."

"Are you going to be upset at me all night?" she asked.

"No, not all night; just until you get here, but I'll get over it. You're right, for my last night here I'd rather hang with you and besides I have a lot of packing to do."

8

Callie was a little sad after dropping Angel off at the airport. They'd stayed up all night talking and drinking and now it was time for her to get back to reality. She was making her way to the production set when her cell phone rang and Abby, one of Cade's assistance was calling her. She answered quickly.

"Hi Abby."

"Callie, hello. I'm glad I was able to catch you early. There's been a slight change in meeting plans for this morning. I've set up some interviews with Cade and his partner for the show to bring on some additional staff. Part of that staff will be a couple of assistants for you and Benji the other stylist. I was able to pull a few resumes from those we already had and we're conducting them at the hotel where Cade is staying. He already has press later at the hotel so it would be a lot for him to leave then return and we can just move the interviews to a conference room there. Is it an inconvenience for you to meet me at the hotel? I've already contacted others from the team who need to sit in on the interviews and they'll be meeting me there."

"No inconvenience at all," she said.

"Great."

Abby gave Callie the address and being only a few blocks away, she turned around and headed in that direction.

She quickly found a parking space in the garage and went up to the lobby to look around for Abby or any other person on the team since she wasn't sure what room the interviews would be in. She spotted her immediately, but didn't see anyone else. She was in a heated discussion with a member of the hotel staff. She walked in her direction, when Abby finally waved her over.

"Thanks for coming. You're the first to arrive and it turns out the hotel staff hasn't set the room up the way I asked them to yet. I also haven't see Cade or his partner Tyler come down from their rooms yet. I know Tyler stayed here last night in one of suites after Cade's party ran late."

Callie stood and watched as Abby tried to reach Cade over and over on his cell phone to no avail.

"I'm going to go up to try and rouse them. Why don't you come with me while we wait for the conference room to get set up?"

Callie was hesitant thinking she shouldn't invade Cade's space since the day before, she'd decline his invitation to the party.

"Maybe I should stay here and wait for the room to be ready."

Abby started moving toward the elevator.

"Nonsense. I'm sure Cade's up and probably just talking with Aaron or maybe he and Tyler got together for an early meeting and Cade doesn't have his phone where he can see that I'm calling. This will only take a few minutes. There is a lot to do today and I'm usually tasked with getting him up and out."

Callie didn't say anything else and followed her into the elevator. She watched as Abby inserted a key and the elevator went straight to the penthouse level. As soon as they exited, they ran into two members of the security detail who were guarding the floor to be sure no one came up who wasn't supposed to.

"Hey Abby," they both greeted.

She greeted them and went right into work mode.

"Where is Cade? He was supposed to be meeting me in the lobby for a production meeting in one of the conference rooms. I've been calling his cell and he's not answering. I came to see if he's forgotten about it."

"He's in the suite and hasn't come out since last night before the party so I'm guessing he forgot."

Abby tried calling his cell again, but he didn't answer.

"I'll go in and see if he's running a little late," she said. Neither guy made a move to stop her since they knew who she was. Callie followed behind her as they reached the door to the suite when it suddenly opened. Out came two women, one was trying with all of her might to cover up her exposed breasts. Callie knew there was no way the small amount of material was going to do the trick. She looked from the women right into Cade's eyes which were wide with surprise when he noticed she was standing there. He looked from her to the Abby and then to the two scantily clad women who were giggling and thanking Cade for a great time.

He never took his eyes off of her as he spoke to Abby.

"Abby, why are you here? Hello Callie," he said, finally acknowledging her presence.

"There is a meeting this morning Cade which it seems you and Tyler forgot about. We're meeting in the big conference room off of the main lobby. I have several people coming in for interviews. I told you we were doing it here because you're set up to do press her in a few hours and this location was more convenient since you wanted new staff on board this week."

They all turned as the two women waved goodbye to Cade and again thanked him for a great party as they were escorted to the elevator by one of the guards. When they were gone, all eyes turned back to Cade who was at a loss for words.

The last thing he wanted was for Callie to see him with two half-naked women leaving his room. He wanted to tell her that the women didn't spend the night with him, but with some friends who were invited to the party and were all too drunk to leave. He allowed them to stay in his spare bedroom and it wasn't until he woke up that he discovered there were women in the other room. Words weren't going to work for this situation, at least not at the moment because when he looked at her, all he saw was disdain, disappointment and disgust. In her eyes, he saw a woman who got an up close and personal view of his life and she didn't like it. If he had any plans of getting closer to her, those plans were just shot down.

"Cade? Did you hear me? Get dressed and get moving. You only have a couple of hours to get through this before you need to change and get ready for the crowd of press coming in later."

Callie seemed to be the only one put out by the scene that just took place with the two women. Clearly everyone but her must be accustomed to what just happened and it didn't faze them. She, on the other hand, was embarrassed to have seen the result of a wild night of partying. She tried to look away from Cade's all-pervading stare as it appeared his mind was searching for words to explain himself. She knew it wasn't the time and decided to go back down to the lobby. Thoughts of what Cade and those women were engaged in taunted her. Why was she so bothered considering she wasn't interested in him? Whatever the reason, she felt uncomfortable standing around.

"I think I'm going to go back down to the lobby. I'll check to see if the room is ready for the meeting and to see if anyone else has shown up yet."

She turned to walk away and as she did, she heard Cade utter that he was sorry in a tone that was full of condescension at himself for the image the whole scene left imprinted on her mind.

She didn't respond, but got back into the elevator without looking back and waited peevishly for the doors to close.

Abby, who had been watching the play of emotions that Cade went through looked at him questionably.

"You want to tell me what's going on here? I sense there is something more going on here than just idle embarrassment of being caught with two women coming out of your room. This isn't news to us so why are you apologizing and why to Callie?"

He didn't answer, but turned around and went back into his suite, sat down and dropped his head into his hands.

"That was stupid of me."

"What was? Apologizing for being you?"

"No Abby. For letting Callie see what just happened. I can only imagine what she thinks took place and it actually didn't. They weren't here with me, but I doubt I'll be able to explain that to her."

"Wait, explain it to Callie? Why would you need to explain it to her? Is something going on between the two of you? If so, you should have told me and I would have known better than to bring her here at all. What are you thinking getting involved with her? You know she works on the set and that could cause major problems with everyone, especially the other women. They all have lust-filled eyes for you and it could make things uncomfortable for everyone, especially Callie. Big mistake Cade. Big, gigantic mistake. Is that why you recommended her as a stylist?"

"You can stop badgering me. There is nothing going on between Callie and me, but I will admit I do like her. I recommended her because she's good and you know that. Don't make up something that isn't there."

Abby for once was silent.

"Yes I did ask her out and she turned me down."

"Whoa, a woman turned you down?"

"Twice," he said holding up two fingers.

Abby beamed.

"I like this woman even more now. Good for her. I told you before to stop messing over these women and find you someone that means something to you. It's time you stopped all this bed hopping anyway. I take it Callie isn't the bed hopping with the sexiest man alive kind of woman."

"No she isn't and I wasn't pegging her as that type. Like I said I like her and I was hoping to get to know her."

"Not after what I just saw."

"What you saw, what she saw is not what happened."

He stood and tried to shake off the feeling that he'll never be able to fix this with her. If she didn't go out with him before today, she never will now after the display of ass and boobs leaving his room. He needed to get himself together. Even though this time he wasn't guilty of indulging in the two women, it showed him how he looked to those around him and that look on Callie's face, he never wanted to see again.

"I'll be ready for the meeting in a few minutes. Check to see if Tyler is still in his room and let him know we're ready. I'll have my guys clear the suite so that housekeeping can get in here."

She got up and looked around.

"Yeah, I hope you realize more than just this room needs to be cleaned up."

He looked at her and wanted to disagree, but he couldn't. She was right.

"I do," was all he said before heading into his room to shower and change.

9

A week had gone by before Cade ventured to the set where he knew he would run into Callie. He spent a few days figuring out how to apologize to her for what she'd seen outside of his hotel suite. That day, once he'd finally gotten dressed and went to the conference room for the meeting, he noticed Callie was unable to look him in the eye. Each time he tried to catch her attention, she would look away and pretend to focus on something else.

He had a plan to try and talk to her before she left, but as soon as the meeting was over, she ran for the door while he got caught in the middle of a conversation with Abby and Tyler about press for the new season of the show. He liked being hands-on, but a lot of the details he was getting more and more involved with he wanted someone else to handle. It was time to get Abby to delegate a lot of his decision making especially on things that didn't need his vote. He missed an opportunity to talk to Callie because of something he no longer cared about.

As he walked around the set as people hustled by he spotted Callie taking measurements for a member of the cast. He didn't want to single her out by giving her too much attention which would cause people to gossip. Thankful for technology, he pulled out his cell phone and did something he should have done days ago and that is either call or text her and apologize. He found a corner where he wouldn't be seen, but where he could still see her and typed out a text. He looked up after hitting send to see her pull out her cell phone. For several seconds she stared at the phone and he assumed she was trying to decide if she should reply or not. He watched her type away and waited for his phone to vibrate. When it did, he smiled and looked down, grateful she even responded.

Callie: There is no need to apologize to me. You are entitled to live your life and do whatever pleases you.

Cade: Seeing the disappointing look on your face didn't please me and for that I'm sorry.

Callie: Again, no need to apologize. I hope your party turned out nice.

Cade: Those ladies were not at the party with me, but with two friends of mine who were staying in my suite in one of the other rooms and yes the party was nice. I actually retreated to my room early and left everyone partying. It had been a long day.

Callie: Oh, okay.

Cade didn't know what to say next. He didn't know why it meant so much to him that she knew what she saw had nothing to do with him.

Cade: I know I'm asking a lot here, but if you have a free moment later, could you give me a call?

He looked up to see if he could garner what her reaction would be, but he couldn't see her face. He watched her pause before she finally typed a message back. It was a short one and he assumed it was another no response with an apology of why she couldn't.

He looked down and saw one word, yes. He typed back a thank you and decided to let it go at that point and not say something stupid that would cause her to change her mind.

Feeling good about himself, he went in search of Abby and Aaron to get to his next appointment.

**

Callie had finally made it back to her hotel suite after a long day on the set. It was after eleven at night and all she wanted to do was get a bath and go to bed. She did remember that she'd promised to call Cade and she hoped it wasn't too late. She didn't know why she agreed and decided to stop dissecting everything. Perhaps he just wanted to talk. She went into the bathroom and ran water for a bath and dialed his number.

"Hello Callie."

"Hi. I hope I'm not disturbing you."

"Not at all. I'm on my way home from a late meeting and was hoping you were still going to call. How did things go on the set today?"

"Things went great and we have a full day of shooting tomorrow. The new assistants that were hired will be starting tomorrow and that will take off some of the load."

"I'm really glad everything is working out for you. I'm also glad you decided to say yes to calling me. I know I've been pestering you about going out for a drink or lunch with me, but I wanted to expound on my apology earlier today. I'm really sorry you saw those women coming out of my suite. I was being totally honest when I said they were not there with me. I know them from other parties, but they didn't spend the night with me. Can I be totally honest about something else?"

"Sure."

"I really hoped you would have changed your mind and come to the party. When I realized you weren't, that's when I decided to chill in my room and avoid the party. There is something about you that I can't shake and it's been eating away at me. I know you probably know that I don't usually have a problem getting women to say yes to me except when it comes to you and it baffles me."

"So do you see me as some kind of challenge where you'll keep trying until you get what you want and then you'll feel like you won; like you are once again Cade Weston the playboy heartthrob that everyone talks about?"

"No, Callie that's not it at all. From the moment I saw you at the airport, there was something about you besides your enchanting beauty that attracted me to you. Once we talked in depth on the plane I became even more fascinated with you and that's something that has never happened to me before. I'm accustomed to having women around a lot and I'm not shy or apologetic about that. After we met and talked, I have wanted to get to know you better ever since and it doesn't matter how many times you turn me down, I still can't back down. It's not an ego thing at all. I really like you Callie and I honestly want to get to know you."

She heard his sincerity and perhaps she was wrong about his intentions of being another man out to bed her and show her to the world as another woman on his arm or another notch on his bedpost.

"Cade I think you're a really nice guy and under different circumstances I would probably enjoy getting to know you, but I have had issues in the past dealing with men I work with and for and I don't want any trouble or gossip following me around. I really like this job and I don't want anyone thinking I got it because there is something personal between us."

"I understand that and I see how the spotlight centers on women who are linked to me and I wouldn't want that for you. I also don't want to miss an chance to really get to know you and let you get to know me. I don't know what impact it will have on either of us, but I hope you'll at least consider it. I know you don't want to be seen in public having a drink or out to eat, but if I can work something out where you wouldn't be exposed to cameras going off or gossip columns writing about you, can I see you outside of work?"

She was tempted and at the same time, afraid of where it could lead.

"How would you plan something like that?"

"Well for starters, why don't you come down to the lobby of your hotel for a few minutes? When you do the concierge will bring you to a private office. I want to see you and I promise I won't take more than five minutes of your time."

A sense of nervousness and excitement flowed through her.

"You're hear at my hotel?"

"Yes. I redirected my driver when you called me. If I could convince you to say yes to a private dinner sometime I wanted to at least be able to say goodnight to you in private. I can't stop thinking about you and that's the honest truth. I haven't seen you in a setting that wasn't work related since we were on the plane. I promise I don't have an ulterior motive; I just want to see you."

"Are you sure there are no paparazzi around anywhere?"

"I'm sure. I can come up through the service elevator straight to the concierge office. He's a friend I play basketball with when I can get a break to play. He's an honest guy and when I call him, he'll think I'm crazy, but he'll help me out in the name of friendship. What do you say?"

She contemplated and then agreed.

"Okay. I'm coming down. How will he know it's me?"

"What do you have on?"

"I'm going to slip on a black sweat suit and red top."

"Okay, take the elevator down and ask for Norm. He'll take it from there. I'll see you shortly," he said and hung up. He dialed Norm, who he knew was working and his friend went in to action to help. He started by making sure no staff were in the area of the service elevator and when Cade got off, he escorted him straight to the office where at this late hour, no one was around. One inside the office, he leaned against the desk and waited for Callie.

He didn't have to wait long when the door to the office opened and she walked in.

"I'll make sure no one comes back this way. Lock the door behind me just to be safe," Norm said before he left.

Cade did and then turned to face the woman who had been invading his every thought lately.

"Thank you for coming down to see me."

"I guess I'm running out of ways to say no to you," she smiled.

Cade wanted to talk, but he also wanted to do something he had been dying to do since the moment he'd met her. He walked over to her and without touching her, he leaned forward and placed a soft kiss on her lips.

"Oh," Callie said feeling an instant electric shock of familiarity when he did.

"Did you feel that?" he asked. He too felt a sense of oneness when he kissed her, as if they were meant to kiss.

"Wow, what was that?"

"I think it was a kiss that was meant to take place since we first met. I've been thinking about it and even though it was short and sweet, it was everything."

Callie's gaze softened and Cade couldn't help the longing he felt to have her close to him.

No one moved or said a word as the world around them disappeared and there was only them. This time Callie didn't wait to be kissed as she leaned into him placing her hands on his chest and gave him an inviting look that encouraged him to go for it again. Her anticipation of what was to come grew when he reached out and drew her close, flush up against him and before her mind could register what was about to happen, he kissed her again and this time it wasn't a soft peck on the lips.

Her breath hitched when he captured and then kissed first her lower lip and then her top before covering her mouth completely with his. When his arms wrapped around her waist, she raised hers up and braced herself by holding on to his shoulders.

The kiss was hot and hypnotic. The more he gave her the more she craved. She wantonly joined him in the kiss as her stomach churned with a need that she'd never felt before. She felt light-headed and dizzy as want zipped through her with a force that took control of her. She kissed him back with a fierceness that made her think that this kiss with him was life. When he withdrew from her, she prayed her heart would slow to a healthier pace.

"Whew! That was some kiss," she said after she could form the words.

"It was a perfect kiss; one I've been waiting a long time to have."

Callie didn't know what to say. Kissing him was enchanting and captivating. Her lips tingled while her breath quickened and if her heart didn't slow its pace, she was going to need to sit down.

"Now that I've gotten that out of the way, let's talk about dinner. I have a house in the hills that's as private as a remote island. The security is tight and you won't have to worry about your place on the job being compromised. I can have one of my friends who owns a restaurant prepare a fabulous meal for us, have it delivered and we can eat, talk, get to know each other, watch movies or listen to music without interruption and without worry. I don't want to pressure you into doing anything other than taking the time to get to know Cade and not just Cade Weston. When you're ready to leave, I'll have either Aaron or Sean on my security detail take you back to your suite. I trust both of them with everything, so don't worry about them or Abby. I kind of mentioned to her that I was interested in you and she knows I was planning to continue to pester you until you said yes. I'm glad it didn't take forever because I was running out of ways to try and convince you," he chuckled.

Callie wanted to see where things could go as well and if they could work it out where they could keep whatever happens between them out of the public eye, she was willing to do it.

"Dinner sounds nice."

"Great. How about this Friday night. I know that taping is wrapping up early because of the late night filming on Saturday."

"Friday sounds like a great idea."

"I don't want to keep you because I know how tiring being on a set all day can be. Thanks for letting me see you. You've just made my night. Why don't you go out first and just keep walking without looking around. I'll wait about ten minutes and have Norm make sure no one is around and I'll slip back out the way I came."

"Okay."

As she turned toward the door, she felt herself

being pulled back into his arms and into another kiss that held the promise that she will have no regrets about getting to know him.

10

Callie changed for the fifth time, uncertain of what to wear. She didn't want to wear anything that seemed inviting or provocative, but on the other hand, she didn't want to be obvious that she was covering up her body to not tip the scales of the direction of her evening with Cade. She didn't know what to expect other than Cade told her the night was in her hands. He left no doubt in her mind that he wanted her, but that he would never pressure her knowing that it was more important to him to get to know her than to get her out of her clothes.

He turned out to be different than she thought he would be. She knew of his playboy ways and the number of women he had been linked to over the years. His parties were legendary around the Hollywood circuit and she had even read sordid stories of women who claimed to have slept with him and gave a play by play of their intimate encounter with him, though not every story can be trusted. She was a testimony to that herself knowing the number of rumors that had been printed about her in the past. She wanted to trust Cade when he said he was developing feelings for her that he'd never felt for any woman before. Tonight she was throwing caution to the wind and will let what is naturally occurring between them happen.

Cade had called her every night since he'd stopped by her hotel and sometimes they talked to the wee hours of the morning. Once during the week, he'd taken a flight to Chicago to do a talk show and had called her to keep him company on the flight.

She admitted there was more to him than what the media portrayed. He was down to earth, honest and best of all, he was all about his family which consisted of his brothers and his grandparents. They had a lot in common.

They both loved chocolate except in ice cream. The shared a love for old black and white movies and the movies, Love and Basketball and Love Jones were each their favorites. He had a stupid love for all kinds of potato chips and she had a thing for popcorn, both having a love affair with salt. He was just as fanatic as she was about working out and they even agreed to work out together sometime.

Tonight they were finally going to have dinner at his house and he had planned everything out from what they would dine on to a few movies he picked out for them to enjoy after dinner. He wouldn't tell her what his friend who owned the restaurant was preparing, but he did ask her for several of her favorite dishes and he would take it from there.

She would feel much better about the night if she could figure out what to wear. She had called Angel earlier in the day to tell her about the date because she was tired of keeping it to herself and she knew Angel would keep her secret. She wished Angel was in California to help her pick out something to wear. As luck would have it, she was thinking about Angel when her ring tone played a Phyllis Hyman classic, Angel's favorite singer. She should have known she wouldn't get out the door without hearing from her.

"Yes Angel, I'm getting dressed, or at least I was before you called interrupting me," she said.

"I know I'm not interrupting you because friends are never an interruption. I want to know what you're wearing for your hot date."

If only she knew, Callie thought to herself.

"I don't know yet. I've gone through several choices and I haven't made up my mind. I don't even know if I should dress casual in some jeans or if I should glam it up."

"Callie, you are having dinner with Cade Weston. He is the hottest man on the planet right now. You need to wear something to knock his socks off and you have plenty of options to choose from. You're in

California where the temperature is two thousand degrees so I say wear white to stay cool. You look fabulous in white and then add accessories in your favorite color, purple. Look at me giving the fashion designer slash stylist clothing advice. I need your job!"

"Sure, that will qualify you. I had a pair of white form fitting capris with my white see through top. I'll add in my pink and purple tank top and purple sling back stilettos. That way I'll be comfortable and the accessories will dress it up just enough that I won't feel awkward if I show up and he's dressed up."

"What did he say he had planned for the evening?"

"That's just it; he didn't say exactly. We are hanging out at his place and getting to know each other. He thought it would be safe to have dinner at his house in the hills. It's pretty secluded and well protected from prying eyes. He's sending a car to pick me up in about an hour. Do you think I'm making a mistake? Am I sending the wrong signal by going out to his private residence? Maybe I should call him and tell him this may not be a good idea."

"Cal, first of all calm down and breathe. I don't think it's a mistake and since you are the one who doesn't want to be seen in public with the sexiest man alive, I'd say having dinner where you won't be seen is a good idea and this house seems like the best plan. Go with it and have a great time. Are you taking an overnight bag?"

"No I'm not taking an overnight bag. I'm planning to come home at a decent hour."

"You will do no such thing. You will allow me to live vicariously through you and you will get us a piece of Cade Weston tonight. I don't know if this is a one-time fling or a budding relationship, but either way, lose the panties tonight".

Callie scoffed at her.

"How is it that we're friends again? What kind of friend encourages another friend to give up the goods on the first date?"

"Girl, I'm the best kind of friend. I give it to you straight, no chaser. It's time you learned to live a little more and I have no doubt Cade Weston is just the man to help you out with that. I've heard stories about his sexual prowess and girl you need to give it a test ride. I don't want to die without knowing what that man is packing!"

Callie couldn't believe the conversation they were having.

"I'm going to act like you're not on the phone trying to convince me to turn into some kind of booty call. I'm going to steer this conversation back to my attire and the fact that I actually like him more than I thought I would. At first I thought he would be another guy trying to get in panties because of his reputation and all, but we have actually spent the week just talking and getting familiar."

"Well yeah, I can see that and now it's time to get extra familiar. Come on girl! It's me you're talking to. You can't tell me you're not interested in something more than just talking and that kiss you shared with him earlier in the week."

That kiss stayed with her for a week. Every time she closed her eyes, she was reliving the moment he touched his lips to hers. Each time, her body tingled and she found herself rubbing her thighs together to ease the ache of wanting more than just a kiss from him. She wasn't sure tonight was the night for that. It was their first date and she wouldn't walk into it with a preconceived notion that it would involve sex.

"Let it go Angel. I'm going to take your advice on the attire and accessories, but I'm saying no to the overnight bag. I have to go because he's sending a car to pick me up and I need to shower and get dressed. I'll call you in a few days."

"You will do no such thing! You will call me tomorrow and you won't leave out a thing! At least take a few condoms just to be safe."

"Bye Angel," she replied before hanging up.

She took a shower, covered her body in her favorite silky soft lotion and quickly dressed after she noticed the time. Sean would be there any minute to pick her up.

She checked herself one last time in the mirror before grabbing her bag. She got to the door of her suite when words from Angel's voice rang in her head. She went back to her room, grabbed a few condoms from her nightstand, just in case, placed them in the bottom of her purse and went out the door. She knew she'd rather be ready than not be.

11

Cade was putting the final touches on his evening with the woman he was becoming obsessed with. Their talks all week had only heightened his interest in her. He'd given his staff the night off so that they would be alone.

Maria and Connie who took care of his home and all of his meals, were given the night off to spend with their families. They were the only two who worked in the evening besides his occasional driver and he had given him the next few days off. Aaron would make sure either he or Sean would be a call away when it came to getting Callie back home at the end of the night.

As much as he would like for her to spend the night with him in his arms and in his bed, he didn't want her to think that was all he wanted from her. He would be a liar if he expressed that he wasn't interested in making love to her. He wanted to badly, but he wanted it to happen when she was ready. He would control his libido for the first time since becoming a celebrity and he would follow her lead. Tonight was about fun and relaxation.

The meal was warming in the oven and because he didn't want anyone on his staff to know of his plans for the evening, he had to set the table himself, with help from his grandmother.

He called her earlier in the week and she'd given him a list of things to set his table up. After compiling the list, Abby had one of his assistance order everything and had it delivered to the house. He'd had Maria do a run to the store and picked up vanilla ice cream, which was Callie's favorite and also had her get a selection of popcorn. He checked everything and then checked it again.

He stopped in his tracks and laughed at himself. This was his first time going all out like this for a woman. He was looking forward to being Cade tonight and not Cade Weston. They should be one in the same, but they weren't. Cade is who he wants Callie to know and enjoy being with. He wanted to leave Cade Weston to the big screen and the Hollywood scene. That's not who he wanted to be around her and he hoped tonight would be more proof to her that she wasn't just a conquest for him; a surprise even to himself.

He was about to pick up his phone to check on how far away Sean was with dropping her off when Sean was actually dialed him.

"Hey Sean."

"We'll be at the house in five minutes."

"Great. I'm coming to the garage to get her. I know Aaron told you to hang around until Callie was ready to go, but why don't you go do something fun and I'll check in with you when she's ready to leave. It'll probably be late, but once you drop her home safely, I won't need you again for a few days."

"Got it."

He hung up and went toward his private garage. There were cement walls all around which made it impossible for even the best and most expensive camera equipment to capture anyone once they were inside.

He opened the door to the garage the moment it opened and the black Navigator truck pulled in. Once the door was again sealed shut, only then did he come around to help Callie get out.

His eyes widened when he saw how exquisite she looked.

"How is it possible that you get more beautiful every time I see you?" he asked.

"Thank you for always noticing," she said getting out of the car.

"Thank you Sean, she said walking toward the house with Cade."

"Yes Ma'am. Mr. Cade will call me when you're ready and I'll pick you up right here."

"Thanks Sean," Cade added and then entered the house, locking the door and setting the alarm.

Before they got too far, he didn't think he could

take another step until he tasted her lips. Without any pretense, he turned her around and pulled her into his arms.

"Hello," he said smiling before he took her lips in a sizzling kiss that set his mind on fire while his body began humming a tune of pleasure at the immediate sweet taste of her. When Callie joined him as their tongues fought to acquire the ultimate pleasure from kissing, he thought he would lose his mind with want. The night hadn't even begun and he was thinking of all the ways he'd like to explore her with his tongue and knew he needed to slow it down.

"Your kisses are going to be the death of me woman!" he exclaimed.

"I'm just as caught up in kissing you as you are in kissing me so you're not feeling like that all by yourself."

"Okay, I promised a fun and relaxing evening and that's what we're going to do."

He turned and escorted her further into the house.

"Cade your house is beautiful. I couldn't see it like I know I would be able to if it were daytime, but from what I could see on the drive to the house, it's incredible. You were right about the tight security. Even though I'm sure the security at the entrance to the property know Sean, he still got the once over pretty thoroughly before they would open the gate to let us in."

"I told you that you'd be safe here with me and you don't have to worry about your privacy. There is no one here tonight, but us. I gave my staff the evening off. I want you to relax and make yourself at home."

"In that case, the first thing I'm going to do is take off these shoes. The high cost of beauty should not be torn up feet from cute shoes," she said while removing her shoes.

"Get as comfortable as you like. I hope you're hungry."

She was.

"I'm starving. What are we having?"

"We're having lobster stuff with crab meat and shrimp, covered in a sauce that's a special recipe of the chef and it's one he won't share with me; believe me I've even resorted to bribery. I know you like seafood and I figured you would like this. Along with it we're having roasted vegetables and a salad. We have his famous homemade apple pie for dessert and of course there is a half-gallon of vanilla ice cream for you to put on top."

Callie smiled realizing he put great thought into the meal, making sure it was all about her. She knew that he loved seafood as well, something else they had in common, and lobster was also one of his favorites.

"Sounds delicious. Before we eat, can I get a tour of this mansion or would it take all night to see it all? Are you sure you live here alone? This place is massive for just one person."

"I do have a live-in chef and four housekeepers, two who live in the house, one who lives on the property and the other lives close by. The two who live in the house are off tonight and went to visit family. I have a driver, besides my security detail and there are several staff who maintain the property. Security is on the property every day all day in shifts. Other than that, the only others who are ever here are my brothers Cameron and Calvin and my grandparents. Cameron is the one I told you is in school in Florida and Calvin is training to be a navy seal, so he ducks in and out whenever he gets the chance to get away and he wants peace and quiet. The house is situated in four different wings. I have the main wing which is what we are in now. Cameron has his own wing and so does Calvin. My grandparents hate the size and prefer to stay in the guest house on the other side of the pool. I can show you that another time if you like."

"So what does a wing of the house consist of?"

He started walking toward the front of the house to begin the tour of his wing, for now.

"Here in my wing, I have four bedrooms, six bathrooms, a gym and a media room on the top level. The level we are on now has a kitchen, two bathrooms a great room slash theater rom, which is where we'll be chilling after dinner. It also has a formal dining and living room. There is a sunroom that's full of books because whenever I do get any down time, I love to read. This level also leads to the garage where we just came in from and out to the pool, basketball court, tennis court and a kennel. I have six dogs, two Yorkies, Lilly and Sasha actually live here in the house. They have a room upstairs, but at night when I'm home, they love to sleep in my room. The others are too big to be kept indoors. There is also a lower level where you'll find my wine cellar, a full bowling alley, movie theater that seats thirty and a game room. A man has to have his video games."

"Now that's something that makes you a normal, regular guy," she giggled. "Men love their games; makes them feel like boys again."

"I don't know about that, but when I have the guys out, we get in serious competitive mode going from game to game."

"This is some house Cade."

"Come on and let me show it to you."

He started on the lower level and made his way to the top floor.

"Who decorated? Everything is incredible!"

"You may or may not have heard of her, but her name is Loren Knight-Bailey. She owns LKnight Designs. She's done work on a lot of homes in this area since she and her husband moved out here. Her husband is part owner in one of the largest African-American owned architectural firms in the country. If you ever need an interior designer, let me know. She has an eye for beauty."

Before going back down stairs, the last stop on the tour was of Cade's bedroom.

"What size bed is that? It's much larger than a king."

"That bed was specially made for me. Being over six feet tall I need something bigger than your average king."

"The color scheme fits you. I was expecting something black or brown like most men tend to like, but your shades of blue works in here."

"I'm glad you like it. Now that we've completed the tour, let's eat because I'm starving."

Callie's amazement of Cade and his life continued to impress her. There was definitely more beneath the surface than just a handsome face and a killer body.

**

After dinner, Cade put on a movie, something starring Mark Wahlberg, a favorite actor of them both and they relaxed in front of the television on a sofa that was more like a bed. They snuggled as the movie began.

Callie was having a great time and if she were honest, she would say the evening was turning out to be perfect. There was more she wanted to know from him about his intentions, but didn't want the relaxed evening to turn into a serious one.

Cade Weston was a man who could have any woman he wanted, yet he was trying to prove to her that he wanted more from her than just her body.

This wasn't the Cade she'd read about and heard about. That Cade was selfish and didn't care about the trail of women he left behind when he tired of one and moved on to the next. She was curious about what made her different.

The movie ended and Cade stood to put in the next one. Now was as good of a time as any to ask some questions.

"Why me Cade?" she asked out of the blue.

She didn't look up at him, but kept her gaze on the television. There was a pause after her question and she thought he either didn't hear her or didn't have an answer. Perhaps he didn't know what she was talking about. She was about to explain herself when he spoke.

"Why not you Callie? I already know that you know you're beautiful so I won't ask that question. What man wouldn't want someone as lovely as you?"

"So this is about sex?" she asked.

He put the movie in and returned to his seat next to her. He didn't like where she was taking the conversation. For the first time for him, being with a woman was not about sex and he needed to make that clear.

"Don't do that. Don't diminish what's clearly happening between us to mere sex. I admit that when I see you, I can't help that I picture you naked and thrashing around under me in pleasure as you scream my name. You have a body that was made for a man to make love to and I'd be lying if I said I didn't want to be that man. What I don't want is for you to think that if I don't get to be that man that I'm not interested in you. Not only is there more to you, but there's more to me."

"You're Cade Weston and you can have any woman you want."

He knew the words and the story because it's what he's heard from everyone. He's Cade Weston and all he has to do is smile at a woman and her panties will fall to the floor. That's not what he wanted from her.

"I know who I am and my celebrity status is not new to me. What is new to me is you and I invited you here not to have sex, but to get to know you. I wouldn't be a hot blooded man if I didn't desire you, which I do. Don't let your mind take you to the countless number of stories printed about me, linking me to one woman or another. Most of who they connect me to isn't true. A lot of those women are just friends and even more are those trying to make a name for themselves and to help them with their careers and to be seen, I agree to be seen with them at parties or walking the red carpet at an event. The bottom line is there is nothing there."

"Thank you for your honesty and thank you for inviting me here tonight."

Cade changed his mind about the movie and wanted instead to dance with her. He didn't mind cuddling with her while watching a movie, but he wanted to hold her in his arms again.

"Do you mind if I turn the movie off for a bit? I want to put some music on and dance with you. I know it's late and you should probably leave soon, but I want to hold you in my arms before the night gets away from us."

Callie nodded her agreement and watched as he got up to turn on some music. As the sweet, soft tone played, she reached her hand out as he reached for her to stand. She went into his arms as they swayed together to the music.

"The first time I saw you, your loveliness blew me away. You had an air about you that wasn't just about your look, but about the confident vibe I got from you. My attraction was instantaneous and it wasn't about the need to help you. I was glad I could and that it was me that you bumped into that day because it's what got me here and I don't want you to think for one minute that my wanting to see you or have you here tonight has anything to do with sex. It's about friendship, trust and going with a feeling that I have that tells me that I should not let you get away. I know you have reservations about what's growing between us, but I'm genuine when I say I'm interested in you and only you. That's not a line to get you in bed; it's a fact and something that I've never said to another woman before, not even to get her in bed. I'm hoping you will consider going along with me on this and seeing what can develop between us. Whatever is floating around in that pretty head of yours that involves anything other than two adults having a relaxing evening tonight and a discussion about more evenings like this, should be wiped away."

Callie didn't know what to say. This is a man that every woman wants and he's talking about something that involves more than just them having a casual fling, something she knew he was known to do. Should she believe he's trying to shed that image for her? If he was truly serious, she would be a fool to not go the distance and see if something special develops between them. She felt the same pull to him the moment they met, but she chalked it up to fascination.

"I liked you the moment we sat on that plane across from each other and you shared who Cade was with me. Before that, I think I was captivated with who you are just like any other woman, so I left it at that. Now that I know there is more to you than being this Hollywood star, I'd like to see where this could lead. I don't want to be one of those women who's hanging around for the benefit of being with Cade Weston. I haven't dated anyone in a while and I've been cautious about anyone in the entertainment industry."

He continued to hold her and swayed to the music while giving her his full attention.

"I don't want you to compromise who you are or what you want in order to be with me. You wouldn't be the strong woman that you are if you did."

"I said that to say this will only work if whatever is going on between us stays between us. I know Aaron, Sean and Abby know, but if we can keep it to them, I'm okay with that. You said you trust them with your life and your secrets and I'm counting on that. Nothing can get out that we're seeing each other. It may benefit you as far as keeping up the playboy, heartthrob image, but it could cripple my career."

"I will do everything in my power to make sure there is no exposure to our time together. We can always do dinner and relax here at my house or if we want to be out and about, I can close down a restaurant or a movie theater by buying it out for a quiet evening. I know a lot of people."

"I don't think we need to do that, but I would love to appreciate more evenings like this. I haven't been this relaxed in a long time and it feels good to let my guard down."

He looked at the time and it was after midnight. He should probably call Sean to come and pick her up.

"It's getting late and I can either have Sean take you back to your hotel or you can spend the night in one of the guest bedrooms and I promise I won't sneak in to try and tempt you out of your clothes. I meant it when I said it's you I want to get to know and when you're ready, we'll go to the next level."

Cade wanted her to believe that he wanted more from her than just her body and having her under his roof and not making an advance was the biggest test of his will-power that he could show her.

Callie looked into his hazel eyes and saw sincerity. Her heart leaped and so did the most intimate part on her body. How could any woman resist giving him anything he asked for when he looked at them with those piercing hazel eyes.

"It is late and if you really don't mind my taking you up on the offer to stay in one of your guest rooms, that will be fine. I should have brought an overnight bag, but I didn't want you to think I had my mind on spending the night with you," she said bashfully.

"Don't worry about it. I have a shirt you can wear and there are fresh linens in all of the bathrooms. Let me text Sean and relieve him for the night."

"Okay, I'll clean up while you do that."

Callie went into action picking up the bowls of popcorn and potato chips, their empty glasses and took everything into the kitchen.

Cade turned off the music and sent Sean and Aaron a text that all was clear for the night and he'd see them in the morning. Both quickly replied back and he turned his phone off and went in search of Callie.

He stood leaning against the wall watching her work putting dishes away looking like she belonged in his house. The vision he saw would normally scare him with other women, but with Callie, he felt like having her here with him was exactly how things were supposed to be and he liked it.

"Are you ready?" he asked.

Callie turned and looked at him. The first thought that came to her mind was that he had no idea how ready she was.

"I sure am," she said following him after he turned out the lights.

As they reached the top level, Callie asked to see the two puppies she heard barking. Cade took her to the room the puppies shared and couldn't believe that the rooms were designed as if they were two children. The room had beds and was full of toys. The gate at the door kept them from venturing out.

"Do you normally let them roam free when you're home?"

"Yes. They run this place whether I'm here or not. They know I'm here so they're itching to break free. They have mattresses right inside my bedroom door."

"Don't punish them because I'm here. Let them out," she pleaded.

He moved to open the gate and realized, he was in trouble because he had a feeling he would never be able to deny her anything.

After he let Sasha and Lilly out, they followed Cade to the room she would be sharing. He showed her where everything was and was about to leave with the two puppies in tow when Lilly decided she didn't want to leave Callie. Callie reached down and picked her up and Cade was amazed at how easily Lilly took to her. They normally liked no one but him.

"She already likes you," he said.

"If she wants to stay in here with me, let her. I don't mind," she said rubbing Lilly behind her ear, already become best friends.

"As if they both aren't spoiled enough. I'll get her mattress and she can sleep by the door. She is not to get in the bed. I see I'm not the only one who thinks you and I are a good idea," he said smiling.

"Thank you Cade for a wonderful evening. I'm glad you're persistent."

"I'm glad you came and getting you to see the real me was worth the persistence," he said before leaning down for a taste of her lips. "I needed that to get me through the night," he admitted, winked at her and then left with Sasha in his arms.

12

Callie tossed in bed in the shirt Cade had given her to sleep in. He was much taller than her and when she put it on, it came all the way down to the top of her calves.

It was the middle of the night and the house was quiet. She looked over the side of the bed at the little Yorkie that followed her into the room and wouldn't leave. The dog was also asleep and Callie couldn't figure out what her problem was. She was tired after the long day she'd spent on the set and then the incredible evening she'd spent dining, dancing and relaxing with Cade. She should be exhausted and sleep should have come the moment she crawled in the bed. The plush pillows, pillow top mattress and down comforter should have been enough to knock her right out, yet here she was, wide away and staring at the ceiling.

After getting her situated in the room, Cade retreated to his own room as she ran a bath. She thought a lot about Cade's words as she soaked in the bear claw tub. When he produced all of the bath essentials that any woman would die for, she knew he saw the look she gave him that said that he must have lots of female guests to have the items on hand. He reassured her that before her, other than family, the only other women who stayed at his house were the wives of friends who stayed at the house with their husbands when he hosted events. He made it clear that he made sure there were plenty of toiletries for anyone who found themselves without. He wanted to be sure she understood there was something special happening between them because not once over the years had he ever had a woman that he'd been intimate with spend the night at his house. Not only did none ever spend the night, but he kept his intimate relationships to his condo, hotels or his other house in Hollywood, but never to his private sanctuary.

That revelation made her feel special and she began seeing him in a different light. His image as a playboy was never going to disappear, but she liked that around her, he wanted her to know that he was putting the playboy façade on the side and he was introducing her to Cade and not just Cade Weston. That meant something to her and he was beginning to mean something to her as well.

Knowing the virile man that he was, she could tell from the hardening of his body while they danced close that he wanted her and if she were real with herself, she would admit that she wanted him just as bad.

"This is crazy," she said out loud. Why should she deny herself and Cade? What was the purpose of going that slow when eventually they would get to intimacy and the way her body felt over-sensitized even when the comforter rubbed against her, she knew she wouldn't make it through the night without some kind of relief. If she really wanted to be bold, that relief was sleeping a room away from her. Why should she continue to torture herself with thoughts of what it would be like to have Cade in bed ravishing her.

She wanted to give in to what she wanted and right now, she wanted Cade. He said if whatever was happening between them went to the next level, it would be her call and she was dialing the phone, metaphorically.

She went first into the bathroom and checked her appearance in the mirror. He hair was wild and she looked like a seductress which was good because that's how she was feeling. She was braless under the shirt and through the thin material she could see the dark round tips of her nipples as they pressed dangerously hard against the fabric. Just the thought of Cade was doing this to her body and she needed relief; the kind that only he could give her. She wasn't foreign to how to pleasure her own body and there were times when she resorted to that in order to keep from making the mistake of making any late night phone calls that were in essence booty calls. Tonight she needed more than self-pleasure; she needed to feel Cade inside of her, going deep until even the best trained eye wouldn't be able to see where she began and he ended.

She tiptoed passed Lilly who was still sound asleep and exited the bedroom, going in search of Cade. She'd never been the aggressor before when it came to initiating sex so she walked toward his room on shaky legs, nervous from her head down to her twitching toes. She grasped the condoms that she remembered to grab from her bag tightly in her hands hoping she wouldn't seem too presumptuous by bringing four of them along with her. Her hope was that the night would be an endless pursuit of one orgasm after another for them both.

She reached his bedroom door which was slightly ajar. Darkness covered the room, but the moonlit night allowed her to see his sleeping figure. Apparently he didn't have the same troubles she encountered trying to usher in sleep.

Before she lost her nerve, she padded across the plush blue carpet toward the soundly sleeping body in the bed. She reached his bed just as her eyes began adjusting to the darkness. She peered down at his handsome face and she knew she'd made the right decision in coming to him.

He was gorgeous even though he was sound asleep. She reached her hand out and ran it slowly down his hairy, chiseled chest. She was glad he hadn't worn a shirt because she wanted a permanent vision of him shirtless planted on her brain. She could see the tops of his pajama bottoms showing just above where the comforter lay across his hips. She was imagining those hips as they pushed his turgid flesh in and out of her body. Her legs began to quiver at the thought and her breath quickened.

"Don't let me stop you," Cade said.

The sound of his voice startled her and Callie snapped her hand back.

"I'm sorry. I didn't mean to startle you," she stuttered through her words.

Cade reached out, pulled her hand and placed it on his chest where it had rested before he spoke.

"You didn't startle me sweetheart. I thought I was dreaming and what a pleasant surprise I got when I opened my eyes and you were standing here enjoying the view.

Callie shivered hearing his deep, heavy, sex-laden toned voice that made her think of seduction at its finest. The darkness heightened her sensitivity to his sound and her fingers twitched nervously at the feel of his placing hers to once against rest on him.

"I couldn't sleep," she admitted. "I'm sorry I woke you up."

"Baby, never apologize for waking me up when you need anything from me. Is there something you need that I can help you with?"

Before she could speak, Cade reached over and pushed a button on the wall beside his bed and the room illuminated in a soft glow from dim lights placed across the ceiling.

She had not looked into his face since he spoke and the last thing he wanted was for her to feel uncomfortable. Even now with the room dimly lit, he watched as she kept her focus on the hand that was now on his chest and he could tell by her rapid breathing that she was nervous.

"Maybe this wasn't a good idea, coming into your room like this," she murmured softly.

"Callie, look at me," he said, not moving afraid she'd lose her nerve and run from the room.

He spoke softly again, hoping to reassure her that anything she felt was okay and she should be free to explore whatever she wanted with him.

"Callie, please look at me," he pleaded.

He watched as she slowly lifted her gaze to his face and what he saw took his breath away. Seeing her standing in his room was one thing, but seeing the look of undeniable desire for him staring back at him was about to cause his undoing. The eyes staring back at him left no doubt that she wanted him and that was her plan when she entered his room.

"Tell me what you need, baby. I'm right here and I want you to feel unrestricted and uninhibited when it comes to what happens between us. I meant what I said when I told you wherever things go with us, it's because it's what you want and not what I want. I never want to assume even if I wake up and find the sexiest woman I've ever met standing in my bedroom in a shirt with her hair all wild and sensual looking with a look that says she's ready to devour me any minute, that what she wants is me."

Now that she was looking at him in the soft glow of the lights, there seemed to be an animalistic vibe in the air that both knew existed. What needed to happen, if she wanted what she came into his room for, she was going to have to say.

"I want you Cade."

He waited to see if she would say anything else and when she didn't, he knew that was all he was going to get out of her. He understood that it took everything in her to make the steps from her room to his and now she wanted him to take over.

He didn't speak as he sat up, pushed the comforter to the foot of the bed and swung his legs out so that they were resting on the floor. He opened his legs and slid back so that he could turn her to sit in between his legs. As her behind slid down into the area between his thighs, he felt her exhale and knew that where she was at first nervous, she was now beginning to relax. He opened her hands to entwine their hands together and he looked down to see that in one of her hands, she'd brought condoms with her.

She looked at him when she remembered she

had them.

"I wasn't sure if we would need these before I got here tonight, but I didn't want to be without them just in case things went there."

"Things are definitely going there and I'm glad you thought of them. I see you have high hopes since it looks like you brought several."

"I'm hoping to use every single one of them," she proudly admitted.

"Anything you want from me you can have. If it's me you want, it's me you will get anytime, anywhere and as many times as you want and need. Never be shy in telling me what you need because whatever it is, especially if it involves us being together like this, then I'll oblige every single time."

Callie clenched the muscles between her leg as pictures of them making love entered her mind and singed through her body.

"I aim to please baby and I have several more in my nightstand just in case we're both feeling extra energetic before the night is over," he quipped lighting the mood a little.

Callie didn't know what to say and was afraid if she spoke the words wouldn't come out right so instead of speaking, she nodded her head.

Cade snuggled up close to her as she leaned back onto his bare chest. He reached out with both arms, encircling her body so that their bodies were completely flushed against each other.

"You smell incredible," he said taking a long

breath in at the nape of her neck. Without hesitation, he slipped his tongue out and ran it along the column of her exposed neck down to her shoulder and back up again placing small, soft, wet kisses along the way. Callie moaned and he intensified his effort while going back down her neck with harder, open mouth kisses as her body became pliant against his.

"I feel good when I'm around you and having you touch me like this is what I want and definitely what I need," she whispered through sighs.

He turned her face around so that they were looking at each other and without words he took her mouth in a tantalizing kiss.

Callie joined in on the assault to her mouth by giving into the kiss that was filled with heat that engulfed her limbs.

"I want to pleasure you in the way you like. Tell me what you like?"

"As long as it's with you, my answer is everything," she replied in a voice laced with passion.

He kissed her again and this time he slipped his hand under the hem of the shirt she was wearing and reached underneath it to cup her breasts making her body wiggle against his as he went between pinching her nipples and caressing them making the tips hard under his touch.

Callie couldn't contain the moans that continued to escape from her mouth as she felt her breasts swell under his ministrations.

"This is only the beginning sweetheart. We have all night to explore each other and right now, I feel like I'm a master of exploration and you have the perfect trails for me to cover."

He continued kissing and licking her neck while slipping one hand down into the front of her panties. He encountered bare smoothness until he reached a thin strip of soft smooth hair that led to the nub that was waiting for his touch. He used his other hand to spread her legs a little for better access and when he encountered a flood of moisture, he stroked her from the hard nub down until he reached the entrance to her womanhood. With one finger, he entered her and Callie almost flew out of his lap when he heard her shriek from the pure pleasure of his touch.

"Cade, I can't take anymore. I need you inside of me, please."

"In time sweetness, in time. I want to feel you come apart in my arms first and I don't want you to hold back. Never hold back when you're with me because as long as you want it, there will always be more."

Callie could feel her hips winding and grinding on their own accord and she was powerless to stop the movement even if she wanted to, which she did not. Cade was doing things to her body that she'd never experienced before. Though this wasn't her first time of being caressed this intimately, he took it to a new level and the feeling was delightful as she was torn between wanting it to go on forever and wanting to give into the feeling and let go of the orgasm that was already threatening to overtake her.

"That's it baby, I want you to enjoy this. Tonight is all about you and getting what you need so let go. I can see your face and seeing you in the midst of pure enchantment is a lovely sight to behold. I can look in your face and tell that you're close to the edge."

"I am Cade, I'm right there, but I don't want to yet. I want to keep feeling like this. Your fingers are magical," she sighed.

"I promise you there will be more," he groaned into her ear, driving her wild.

No more fighting the inevitable he thought to himself. Needing to finally watch her let loose in his arms, he increased the number of fingers inside of her from one to two and at the same time, he used the fingers of his other hand to caress the hard, protruding nub and she plunged off of the ledge of desire and into bliss screaming out her pleasure, no longer able to contain it.

"That's it baby, give me everything you have," he said increasing the pressure of his strokes even more.

He continued to caress her thighs and reached up to caress her arms while soothing her heated body with kisses as she cried out in hunger for him.

Before she could gather her thoughts, Callie felt her arms being lifted as Cade removed the shirt she was wearing bearing her body for his perusal.

Cade wasn't sure she could stand so he lifted her from her sitting position between his legs and laid her out across his bed. When she opened her hooded eyes he saw her need for physical contact matched his own. He stood and reached to remove her now soaked panties from her body leaving her completely naked before him.

"You are truly a lovely woman Callie. I don't want you to think I'm saying that because you're in my bed naked, but because I already knew that you would be even before I saw you like this. Having you here with me is more than a dream come true, but it's the best dose of reality I've ever received. The reality is this is only the beginning of things for us and beyond this night, there is much more to come."

Cade removed his pajama bottoms and reached into his nightstand for a condom. He had placed the one's Callie had brought with her on the nightstand and looking at them, he knew they wouldn't be big enough. When he turned back around, he looked at Callie when she gasped. He watched where her eyes were focused and he smiled.

"What I bought with me was a waste I'm sure. You are definitely packing more than what a regular size condom would hold."

He knew of his large size and his plan was to take things easy so that he didn't hurt her.

"Whatever my size, we're going to make this work because there is no way I'm not getting inside of you tonight."

"I think it's going to take some work to make that happen. Will I be able to walk in the morning?" she laughed, glad that things were not awkward between them.

Cade smiled back at her while he took the time to cover his massive length and girth and then joined her on the bed sliding her legs open as he kissed his way up her body.

"Baby, if you can't walk, I'll carry you wherever you need to go as long as I can get in you before I have a heart attack from desire for you."

"I'm serious Cade, you do realize you are much larger than the average guy and I happen to be the size of an average woman. I'm feeling anxious and nervous at the same time."

"I promise if you try me on for size, you'll see it's a perfect fit."

She didn't get another word out as he covered her mouth with his while straddling above her not putting his full weight on her. The kiss stole every ounce of energy she had. His kisses were aggressive and demanding and she gave as much as he was giving to her. The kiss continued as her senses went on overdrive at the feeling of him sliding her legs open wider and planting himself right in the middle. She opened them willingly ready for his entrance into her body.

"Are you ready for me baby," Cade said as he leaned down on her body and aligned his pulsing erection to the center of her. Before going in, he rubbed himself up and down the cleft at the apex of her thighs and when he couldn't take anymore, he pushed slowly into the core of her which was dripping wet with her essence.

"Yes," she was able to get out on a sensual moan as she felt the tip of him begin to enter her. He was large and she hoped the pain of the first entry was lessened by the intense feel of him once he was deeply seated in her.

She felt his hips sway back and forth in short, slow penetrating thrusts as he pushed in slowly and then withdrew before going back in again giving her a little more of himself with each pass in. Feeling the size as he tried again and again to enter her body made her involuntarily tense up, afraid of taking him all in.

"Don't tense up baby," Cade said through clinched teeth as he tried to hold on to some semblance of control.

"One thing I know for sure is that you and this body were made just for me and we will fit together perfectly. Relax and open up for me."

She did as he asked and relaxed because she wanted him just as bad as he wanted her. When she did, she felt him withdraw and push back in again and this time he did enter her all the way to the hilt where he then stopped moving.

"Baby, are you alright?" he asked.

"Mmm, yes. I'm better than ever and I'll be even better when you start moving again."

Cade didn't need more of an invitation than that. He pulled himself out and in one long swoop, he entered her body again and this time his entry was met with a vivacious scream of pleasure from Callie's lips.

He rocked into her, finding the right angle for his powerful thrusts, giving her everything she needed and all that he needed to receive. Their slick bodies joining together over and over were the only sounds heard in the room.

Her screams of pleasure urged him on as he loved her. He watched as her eyes closed and her mouth opened while her body was thick in the throes of a powerful orgasm.

In a gruff voice full of hunger and thirst, he finally gave into the pleasure his body sought deeply planted in hers and with his body throbbing and pulsing out of control, his release blindsided him as it slammed into him over and over as if it would never end.

As the pulses lessened and his breathing returned to normal, he placed soft kisses across her face as she mewed like a satisfied cat.

"That was amazing Cade."

"The first word that comes to my mind is earth-shattering. I knew we would be perfect together," he said, taking her face into the palms of his hands, drawing her to him and kissing her with everything in him. Callie met the kiss with unrestrained passion as she let him know that being with him was incredible.

Cade rolled over bringing her with him until they were side by side. He didn't want his weight pressing into her because his body felt like a lump of clay. He worked breaths in and out as he tried to get his body to calm down after that eruption that zapped every out of him.

He reached down, drew her hands to his face and kissed each fingertip, sucking them into his mouth one at a time.

"You are remarkable," he said when he could finally breathe again. "When I can move and breathe at the same time, I can't wait to have you again."

Callie smiled because she was thinking the same thing.

13

Callie woke in a cocoon with a lovely ache in between her legs, a feeling she never wanted to go away because it was a reminder of the night before that had been playing over again and again in her dreams while she slept. Cade was an amazing lover and never before had she spent a night with a man where she couldn't get enough. The more he gave her the more she wanted. She lost count somewhere in the early morning hours of the number of condoms they'd gone through. His stamina was a test for her and she was happy that the hours she spent each week working out helped her keep up with his ferocious appetite.

She felt good wrapped in his arms and she tried not to move, not wanting him to take his arms from around her. She slid back to get as close to him as she could and her breath hitched when she encountered a fully aroused Cade.

"Oh," she exclaimed quietly not sure if he was

awake or if his body unconsciously reacted to her closeness.

"Oh is right," he responded. "I can't believe after the workout you gave me all night that first thing this morning, as soon as you rub against me, my body responds with a need that can't be quenched and I am not complaining."

He snuggled up against her and placed a soft kiss on the back of her shoulder.

"Good morning," he said.

"Good morning to you and if last night was any indication, it seems that I'm about to have a very good morning."

Cade reached behind him for a condom, hoping he still had one left after using more than he thought they'd use the night before. He grabbed what he could tell was the last of the pack, opened it and quickly sheathed himself.

"I'm about to make this a good morning for us both," he said sliding back over behind her.

She tried to turn around so that she was facing him, but his hand stopped her.

"The feel of you against me in this position has all kinds of ideas floating around in my head and you like this is what I need and at the same time, you'll get your need met."

Callie enjoyed his soft touch as he reached down and gripped then caressed the sweet, sexy, hourglass curve of her behind.

She cocked her head to the side and looked back

as he lifted her right leg up in order for him to easily slide into her already slick passageway. Her eyes never left his as her body focused on the exuberant feel of his going all the way in with a determined thrust. His power surge into her caused her to moan loudly and she closed her eyes to tuned out everything around her except for the feel of him large, long and thick, touching every vessel that caused her body to shiver.

Cade's need to mate with her in a rhythm that was as old as time took over and he plunged into her all the way and then pulled out until only the tip of him remained inside.

"Hold on baby!" he shouted as he pushed forward then out again repeating the rhythm. He felt the drive to give her even more when she used her hand to cover his which was still gripping her hip, bracing them both to keep them from toppling off of the bed to the floor. Her sighs and moans invigorated him, giving him the encouragement to not slow his thrusts. He put his power into giving her all of him as she happily joined him by pushing back into his powerful lunges.

Cade leaned into her ear and sucked the lobe into his mouth again and again before releasing it.

"I feel you," he whispered into her ear. "I can tell you're close and so am I. I want you to come with me Callie."

Callie didn't need much urging when suddenly she exploded with a powerful orgasm so strong, she thought she heard sirens in her head and saw flashes of light across her eyes, reminding her of fireworks exploding in the sky. She continued to ride him adding her own thrusts to the mix as she concentrated on the explosion he too was racing toward. Immediately following her peak, she felt him let go and screamed his pleasure into the crook of her neck all along never stopping his forceful thrusts into her and unlike anything she'd ever experience before she felt another orgasm rising in her. Before she had a chance to assess what was happening, she again shattered into a million pieces as wave after wave came over her again. She screamed his name because no one but him has ever made her feel the way she was feeling at the moment.

After they crested and were now coming down from the pinnacle of pleasure, they collapsed as bliss filled their bodies and minds.

Cade drew her to him and they stayed that way until their bodies cooled down.

"As much as I am enjoying being here with you I have to go and I mean very soon. Isn't your staff going to show up some time soon? We can't risk them seeing me here."

She tried to move, but Cade pulled her back toward him.

"Whether my staff is coming or not, that doesn't mean you have to leave."

Callie turned around to face him. She relished in

the moment which seemed surreal. She was naked and in bed with Cade Weston, a place women would scratch her eyes out if they thought they could replace her. His handsome face was beckoning her to kiss it and she did.

She first started with his lips and when he tried to take the kiss deeper, she pulled back and sucked on his bottom lip before caressing it with her tongue. She moved her lips to his cheek and then to his chin before placing one more soft kiss to his lips.

"The less people who see us together, the better things will be. You know how this has to be. I need to go before anyone gets here."

She started to move and remembered she didn't drive her car and she turned back to him.

"I forgot I didn't drive here."

When she spoke Sasha started barking, no doubt needing to go out.

"I see you're not the only one who needs out of here," he said.

Cade did move then and reached for his cell phone dialing Aaron. After giving him instructions to send Sean with one of the vehicles to pick her up, he followed her and got up out of bed.

Callie turned and watched as he searched for his pajama bottoms. When he stood up her eyes went straight to his crotch where he was removing the spent condom and threw it in the trash with the rest they'd gone through since their night began.

"See something you like?" he asked jokingly.

"I do and I did like it very, very much," she replied smiling like a woman who'd just won the lottery.

"If I had any more condoms left, I'd entertain seeing how much more like you could get out of it."

"It's not my fault you have an insatiable sexual appetite."

"Well you didn't complain each time I took one off to put on another one."

"I wouldn't complain if you had more condoms left either which is even more reason for me to leave right now. I see that look on your face and it's not happening. I'm going to get a shower while you take the puppies out."

The grin on his face was of a man who was planning to join her in the shower.

"Don't even think about it. I'm taking a shower alone while you figure out how to get me out of here without anyone seeing me."

Cade walked around the bed to come face to face with her.

"I hope you had an enjoyable evening with me and I'm not speaking only of the sex. I enjoyed getting to know more about you and I hope I can see you again."

"I will answer that as soon as you do me one favor," she said.

Cade looked at her quizzically.

"I need you to put some clothes on. I know you

know what you look like and I see why they call you Heartthrob. A girl can only resist so much and you Mr. Weston are irresistible."

Cade looked down and realized he had not put his pajama bottoms back on. The image of her not being able to resist him had his penis jump with a need for her.

Callie whistled at him.

"If only I had the time," she said quietly, but not quite enough that it would escape his ears.

"When you do have the time, I'd like to know what you'd do."

She laughed and covered her mouth.

"I didn't realize you could hear me."

"I heard every word and believe me there will never be a time when we'll run out of condoms again, that is if you'll answer my question about seeing you again."

She knew she shouldn't. She'd gotten her itched scratched over and over again and she knew she should stop now, but looking at him standing before her with his hairy muscled chest, sexy dimples and artfully structured piercing hazel eyes, she knew there was no way she could walk away and not see him again.

"My answer is yes."

Cade smiled like a kid in a candy store as he finally put on pants.

"Sean will be here soon to take you back to your hotel. Don't worry about anything about the night we spent together getting out. I know your privacy means a lot to you and I want you to trust me with knowing that."

Callie came up to him on her way to the shower.

"I do and thank you. I'll be ready in a few minutes," she said, kissing him one last time on those lips she couldn't seem to get enough of and went into the bathroom.

"Are you sure I can't join you for your shower?" he asked, adding in a pout.

"Not this time, but I promise I will give you a rain check."

"Whew! I am looking forward to that rainy day!" he exclaimed watching her as she entered the bathroom with a behind that dreams are made of.

He got busy straightening the bed as best as he could. Maria, one of his most trusted employees would come along in a little while and straighten up and change the linens. In the meantime, he grabbed the trashcan to dispose of the used condoms. That was something he didn't want anyone else to be responsible for but him.

While he waited on Callie, he went into one of the other bathrooms to shower and change so that he could escort her to the car once Sean showed up. He stepped into the shower and turned on the steaming hot water and when thoughts of Callie in the shower a few feet away crept into his head, he turned the water on cold so that the coolness would put his rising arousal to rest.

"You heard her say no, so get yourself together," he spoke down to his penis which seemed to have a mind of its own. He was feeling extra chipper when he noticed he was whistling.

"Why the hell am I whistling?" he asked himself. One thing was for sure, the night he'd just spent with Callie was the most memorable he'd ever experienced with a woman.

He showered quickly and after grabbing sweats, he went in search of Callie. When he reached his room she was putting on the last of her clothes just as his cell phone rang signally Sean had arrived.

"Sean's here."

Callie followed him down the hallway in the opposite direction that they'd come in to get to the bedrooms the night before.

She smiled when he grabbed her hand into his as they walked.

"There is an elevator at the end of the hall of the next wing of the house that goes straight to the. It's the only one that does. I'll take you down."

"Thank you for a wonderful evening and morning."

He was glad to hear she'd enjoyed herself.

"I'm glad and like I said, I really want to see you again. Maybe we can actually go out someplace to dinner."

"You mean out in public? We can't do that and you know it."

"Okay, I'm not going to have this argument with

you about those you work with thinking you're getting ahead because of me, at least for now."

They stepped into the elevator and as soon as the doors closed, Callie felt herself being pulled into his strong arms and kissed passionately, barely giving her a chance to breathe.

She leaned into him loving the warm, soft yet hard and demanding touch of his lips to hers. When his tongue went in search of hers they began a tango that stole her senses. When the doors opened, they slowly broke apart, each breathing like they'd just ran a marathon.

"Your lips do wild things to me."

Cade came close to her lips.

"The next time I have you naked and in my arms, I'll show you what else these lips can do. You haven't experienced my wildness yet."

The heated flare in his hazel eyes made her gasp. She had a feeling he meant every single word.

"Until next time," she said.

"Yes, until next time."

Cade walked her to the waiting black truck.

Sean stepped out as they approached.

"Sean, see that she gets to her hotel safe and use the private entrance," he instructed.

Sean acknowledged and after making sure Callie was comfortably seated in the back, he got in and took off.

Cade watched until the garage door opened and closed and then he retreated back into his home.

As he took the elevator back up to his room to prepare for his busy day, Aaron's words played around in his head. He wouldn't admit it yet, but Aaron was right. Callie was about to be a part of their lives and he feared his heart was in trouble.

14

Callie had been busy working and going to interviews for additional work on a few new projects she'd been hearing about.

She hadn't had a chance to talk to her since the day of her dinner at Cade's house and Angel had left several messages still asking about that night.

She was glad Angel popped into her head because she needed to talk to her. She checked the time and with the time difference, Angel would be in her office at work.

"Hey girl!" Callie shouted when Angel answered.

"Hey yourself. You should be ashamed of yourself keeping your best friend waiting on pins and needles to hear about your dates with Mr. Heartthrob. Now that you've finally found a free moment to talk to me, tell me everything and don't you dare leave anything out."

"Angel, I'm not going to tell you everything; only those things I think would be fun to tell you."

Callie had to hold the phone away from her ear as Angel shrieked with excitement.

"He rocked your world didn't he? So tell me how is he? Is he as good as reports in all those sleazy magazines say he is from all of the women who can't seem to keep their mouths or their legs closed?"

Thoughts of Cade gave her a warm feeling from head to toe and especially in between her legs. It had been a week since she'd seen or talked to Cade. She was busy and she knew he was as well, especially with his record label. The announcement had come out that several of his artists were nominated for some of the biggest categories in music for the biggest music awards show of the year. Cade's record label had also garnered a nod for record label of the year, a new category being introduced. She had no doubt he would win since his label was putting out one hit artist after another. The top four spots on the most popular charts were all from his label.

"I don't know or care what those magazines say and I'm not telling you anything other than yes we had a nice time together and it involved us being naked, but that's all you get."

"Some best friend you are. If you can't tell me all of your deepest, darkest and hottest secrets, who can you tell? Do you have any idea what it means that my best friend is bumping and grinding with the hottest man on the planet? Every woman of any age would give up everything to hit the sheets with Mr. Heartthrob Weston."

"Every woman Angel? Would you?" she asked lightheartedly.

"Girl, I would kill you and hide the body to get to that brother!" she bellowed.

They laughed in a fit of snickering back and forth.

"You are out of your mind Angel."

"I know and I can only be like this with you. You know I'm happy for you because underneath all that sexiness Cade Weston oozes on the regular, I hear he is a pretty decent guy."

Callie could attest to that. She knows he's a good actor and could play any part, but she got the feeling that their time spent together was just as special to him as it was to her; at least she hoped so. Those hopes were dashing more and more each day when she didn't hear from him.

"That he is girl. He told me a lot about his childhood and his brothers and the fact that his grandparents raised him after his father passed away and his mother disappeared. We talked about all of his business ventures and I shared with him my dreams of being a top designer one day and having the top models in the world walking the runway in my designs."

"I plan to be on the front row cheering you on. I'm already claiming that for you."

"You know I appreciate and love you for always

being in my corner. Anyway, I don't want to keep you long. I wanted to let you know that I'll be done this week with all of the designs of the dresses for the wedding including yours. I need to get everyone measured and then I'll get my seamstresses working on them. I'm coming to Texas in a few weeks and we can take care of everything then. I'll email everyone what they'll look like as well as the three color samples you wanted me to find for you. I think they'll go together good."

"I'm so excited hearing that. I know we still have a few months for the wedding, but it looks like it's coming up fast. Thank you for being my maid of honor. Maybe you can bring Cade to the wedding as your date."

Callie knew that wasn't happening.

"I doubt it Angel. We're not really dating. I'm not sure what it is other than we enjoyed each other's company and had some really, really good sex."

"I knew it! I bet he's packing too isn't he? Come on tell me?"

"I'm not telling you anything. You don't see me asking you about DeWayne and how much he's packing do you?"

"Girl, you can ask and all I will say is it's a good things he's rich. Not that I'm not satisfied because I am and on a regular, but let me just say the money makes up the difference."

Callie laughed. Leave it to her best friend to be

crass without missing a beat.

"Too much information Angel. If Cade wasn't who he was I would probably share more and it's not that I don't trust you. I don't know what this is right now and for the moment, I'm just going to leave it at I had a good time with him and he wants to see me again, though you wouldn't know it since I haven't heard from him in the week since I was at his house."

"What do you mean you haven't heard from him? Nothing at all? Not even a text?"

Callie wished she'd never said anything, but now it's out.

"Don't read too much into it Angel. It's nothing really. He's a very busy man. Remember this is Cade Weston we're talking about. He's got a lot going on every day and I know you've heard about the press his record label is getting now that the music award nominees have been announced. He himself was nominated for his label so all the press he's been doing the past week has taken him all over the world. Listen, we had some fun and that's all it was. If we see each other again, I'm sure it will be fun then too and if not, at least I got an itch scratched that millions of women in the world wish they could."

Callie spoke the words and tried to make herself believe them while she was hopefully convincing Angel to not make a lot out of it.

"I'm not going to say anything because it's your

life. Just be careful Cal. I know he pursued you and gave it to you good and all, but remember he isn't labeled as a playboy for nothing and that nickname, heartthrob, I'm sure means he's left a trail of broken hearts. Just don't be one of them, okay?"

Callie pondered that thought and knew the last thing she wanted to do was be grouped in with a bunch of women that Cade bedded and moved on from. She had to keep it light knowing there were no promises made other than having a good time and she definitely had that.

"I hear you Angel and don't worry about me. I'll be fine. I'll call you next week with my travel plans for coming home. I'll only be able to get away for a few days so carve out some time for a girl's night out."

"Whoo-hoo!" Angel hollered. "You already know I'm making plans. I'll talk to you later."

Callie hung up and her cell phone beeped letting her know she had a text message. She looked at it and it was from one of the production assistants on the show who was sending out a mass text to everyone who worked on the television series she worked on, telling them to turn to the entertainment channel because Cade was on talking about the show.

She grabbed the remote, turned on the television and surfed until Cade's handsome face showed on the screen. Her heart pumped faster in her chest as she marveled at how sexy he looked in all black. He was at a press event and a reporter asked him about the television show. She sat glued to the television as she was sure every hot blooded woman in the world was doing. The television camera loved Cade and even with as good as he looked on the screen, nothing compared to Cade Weston in the flesh and she meant that literally since she knew first hand. Even now her body remembered all of the ways he'd pleasured her and though he was thousands of miles away in another country, she wanted him.

After the interviewer moved on to ask some questions of one of Cade's artists who had accompanied him on the press tour, she watched him take out his cell phone and pecked away on it. Seconds after he finished and lifted his head, her cell phone pinged. She grabbed it and smiled when she realized he was texting her.

Cade: I was thinking about you and wanted to say hello. Sorry I haven't been in touch, but this schedule Abby has me on for press for the television show and the record label has me exhausted. How are you? Are you walking okay these days?

Callie smiled then laughed as he made reference to their wild night of sex when she wondered if she'd be able to walk afterwards. She typed back her reply.

Callie: I'm walking fine now, but that first day I needed an extra soak in the tub when I got home.

You had me using muscles I didn't know existed. You definitely brought the animal out in me.

Cade: Well I'm hoping to bring that animal out for another visit. I'm heading back to California after this last press conference in Dubai. I want to see you when I get back. Is that possible?

Callie: Yes that's possible. I have a lot going on, but I'd like to see you too.

Cade: Good to know. I'll be in California for two days before flying to New York for business. I don't want to take you away from any work you have going on, but can you squeeze out a day? I want you all to myself for a full day with no interruptions.

Callie: I'm not the one with the busy schedule and assistants calling every five minutes. What day are you coming in?

Cade: I'll be home in three days.

Callie: I can make it happen. You do realize the world can see you texting to me right? I'm watching you right now on television.

Cade: It's a good thing there's a wall behind me and no cameras can see what I'm typing or they may see me say that I can't wait to get you naked so that I can take in that magnificent body of yours again. It's been in my dreams since I last saw you.

She blushed even though no one was around to see how embarrassed she was. Cade talking about her being naked had her thinking of him the same way and remembering what she saw when her eyes perused down to his crotch had her crossing and uncrossing her legs to relieve some of the aching she was experiencing where moistness was already forming.

Callie: Tell me when and where and I'll see what I can do about turning your dreams into reality.

Cade: Grab a pen.

Callie searched her bag for a pen and wrote down the address to the hotel where he would be staying for the two days. He would usually stay at his condo, but he already knew the media would be stalking him there and he agreed to respect her privacy and not have her involved in any scandal when it came to them being seen together. He let her know that Sean would be picking her up and that he would get a separate room for her. He told her to check-in early, at least a day before he arrives. If she arrived after him, there was a chance media outlets would find out he was there and follow him around and he didn't want her to be caught on camera at the same hotel.

When they were done, she turned back to the press conference and watched the grin on Cade's face hoping it was because they were going to see each other again. If there was a camera on her face right now, she would be sporting the same grin and for the same reason.

15

Cade was happy this leg of his press junket was over, at least for a few days. He was looking forward to some down time before heading to New York to do more press. He was hoping to spend the little free time he had with Callie. Even now, he should be looking over the manuscripts of the two movie roles he'd recently agreed to do. One was an action flick to be filmed in Monaco. The other was being shot in Miami, one of his favorite cities.

He needed and wanted a slower paced life and even though he'd spent time with countless women in the past, it wasn't until he'd met Callie that he started having thoughts of romantic getaway trips away from the Hollywood scene and weekend trips secluded in his favorite cabin in Paris. Before her, every plan he made was about business.

"What are you daydreaming about dude?" Aaron asked as their flight out of Dubai was taking off.

He shook off thoughts of romance and snapped back to the present with Aaron sitting across from him.

"What? I wasn't daydreaming."

Aaron laughed.

"You sure were and I want to know what gives?"

He started to lie, but decided against it. That was something he never had to do with Aaron. He looked around to see if anyone else on the team, who were on the private jet with them, was in close proximity and would hear his response.

The plane had just taken off and Abby was asleep. The other three members of his security detail had headphones on and his stylist, groomer and two other assistants were all talking in the front of the plane. He sat back feeling comfortable that no one could hear them.

"It's Callie. I cannot stop thinking about her."

Aaron nodded figuring she had something to do with Cade's mystique look.

"So I take it the other night went well?"

Cade rubbed his hand down his face, an expression that he himself was baffled by this feelings about that night.

"Man, she is incredible. I'm saying ou spent hours talking sharing our goals and dreams. I have never felt as comfortable with a woman as I did talking to her. You know how I'm always saying I get a vibe from women immediately that they want something from me, like they have an ulterior motive for being with me?"

"Yeah."

"I didn't get that from her. She seems honest and open and hearing her talk about where she wants her career to go was impressive. She wasn't saying it in a way as if she wanted me to make it happen for her. She is all about making it on her own talent and you've seen her designs. They're incredible and I can see her making it big one day. She talked about her family and hearing her talk about her parents reminded me of my love for my grandparents. We laughed, we joked and we danced. I was definitely Cade that night and not Cade Weston, the playboy or Mr. Heartthrob like the media has labeled me. I didn't pressure or invite her over to get her in bed. I wanted to get to know more about her and I did that."

Aaron sat straight up in his chair, leaned over and whispered so no one could hear him.

"Wait, are you saying you and Callie didn't?"

Cade leaned in as well.

"I'm not saying that because we did and it was out of this world. I saw stars, man. That night was a first time experience for me and you know how many women I've been with. This was nothing like anyone I've ever been with."

"Was that her you were texting during the press conference? You had a stupid woman-crush look on your face with a crazy ass smile while you were typing."

Cade shook his head knowing if anyone caught something strange about him, it would be Aaron.

"Yeah. Before I go to New York, I'm going back to California for two days to see her. I haven't seen or talked to her since that night until the conference today."

"You didn't even call her the next day or anything?"

Cade looked perplexed.

"No. I did what I always do which is jump back into Cade Weston. You know how my schedule has been this week; I haven't had time to do anything other than catch a few hours of sleep."

"What do you want from Callie? Is she a booty call or are you looking at this being something you want to invest time and energy into? I'm telling you I don't think she's the booty call type and according to you she's special and certainly different than other women you've been with. If you want more than just sex whenever you can fit her in, you can't wait a week after you spend the night with her to call or reach out to her. I see you have a lot to learn my playboy friend!"

Cade laughed and sat back in his seat.

"I know I need to re-train my mind when it comes to her. Other than for great sex, I've never wanted to see the same woman over and over again, but I do with Callie."

"That's good to hear. What kind of plans have you made and am I going to have to play mission impossible to get her to you without her being seen?"

"I had Abby get my usual suite at the Montage Beverly Hills. I also had her book a room for Callie. The room is in Abby's name along with several other rooms just to keep people away from the floor. Callie should be checking in later today or tomorrow and when I get there, she just needs to come to my suite. For the two days I'm in town I don't want any visitors and no phone calls unless they are from my brothers or my grandparents."

Aaron sneered.

He caught it and gave him a questionable look.

"This sounds serious Cade."

"For now it's not, but I can say I'm not getting to her quick enough."

"Damn! Whipped after one night. She must have really put it on you and I'm not just talking about sex."

He didn't respond because he didn't want to admit anything yet. He wanted to see Callie and he wanted to see her badly and for the first time in his life, he was admitting that to himself. He wanted to get her in his arms again.

**

Callie had all of the necessities she would need for spending a day or maybe two days with Cade. Now that she had a team working under her on the show, she was able to explain to them what she needed done and told them she had another engagement and wouldn't be around for taping. No one questioned her knowing that she had several jobs going on at once.

After getting the text from Cade, she'd left her hotel to go shopping for something extra special for him. Back when Angel was in town, they'd done some shopping and she remembered seeing a red two-piece panty and bra set. The bra piece was red and sheer and even in her bra size which was a thirty-two double-d, she knew it wouldn't cover her breasts completely, but it covered where she wanted it to and left a lot for his perusal. The panty part could barely be called a panty. It was also red and sheer and was held together at the hip by two black bow-ties on each side. She was glad she'd always prided herself on working out and staying in shape and her figure showed it.

She made sure she packed all of her bathing essentials and included a special body oil just for Cade. She wanted to help him relax after a busy week of press and she knew just how to do it. Once heated, the oil would soothe and relax him and she wanted to be sure she did everything to take his mind off of everything except the way she was going to make him feel.

She wasn't sure what he was planning for them to eat, but when Abby called with the arrangements, she asked her to have fruit, cheeses, crackers and some wine delivered to last the two days. She asked her for Cade's favorite restaurant and after Abby gave her the details, she had her order a meal fit for a night of seduction. Everything would be delivered to her suite and once Cade arrived, she would have his team take everything to his room. She didn't want the hotel staff to get a whiff of anything going on in his suite.

Abby was putting everything in place the way she asked and she asked that the bill be sent to her. Cade, of course, is a very rich man, but she wanted to do something for him. She wasn't as well off as he was, but she could definitely afford to spend a night or two spoiling him.

She hoped she wasn't doing too much or being presumptuous about what Cade had planned for their time together. She liked that he took the time to have everything planned out for them the night she's spent with him at his house and she wanted to return the favor. Now all she had to do was get dressed. Within the hour, Sean would be at her hotel to pick her up and she wanted to be ready. She would wear jeans and a pink tank top and her favorite pink high heeled sandals to the hotel and then change into a pretty little red dress she'd brought with her from New York. The dress was form fitting and sexy and underneath, she would have on the sexy underwear she bought just for him.

Thoughts of Cade included unadulterated images of his slender hips and strong, muscled, bowlegs. The thought of seeing him naked standing before her had her mouth watering with anticipation. She was already imagining the power behind his strong thighs as he thrust into her over and over making her appreciate the male specimen more and more. Everything about Cade screamed sex and she guessed that's how he acquired the nickname, heartthrob, because every time a woman looked at him, her heart would beat profusely in her chest, throbbing with a need to be close to him.

Even as she tried to zip up her jeans, her hands shook with a nervous anticipation of what she'd do the moment she saw him. She was more than ready for him to return.

16

Cade's plane landed and as he exited the plane, the California heat greeted him as he rushed to get into the air conditioned truck. While Aaron and the others on his team gathered his luggage and made sure everything was secure, he took a moment of being in the car alone to call Callie.

"Hi Cade."

"Hi there. I just landed and on my way to the hotel. Where are you?"

"I'm here in my suite waiting on you to get here."

"You sound sexy and I'm sure you look just as sexy. You didn't unpack in your suite did you? You know that was only to be sure you weren't noticed and would be connected to my stay there. I want you with me the whole time I'm there."

Callie breathe a sigh not only loving the deep, smooth, sexy sound of his voice, but hearing that he was just as anxious to see her as she was to see him.

"No I didn't unpack. My luggage is still at the

door to the suite. I'll be here until you let me know you want me to come to your suite."

"I'll send Aaron for you when I get there. Do you have any plans for today and tomorrow while I'm here where I'd need Aaron or Sean to get you in and out?"

"No. I'm all yours."

"Don't make me have my driver run red lights to get to you with the visual you just gave me of you being all mine. I'm going to hold you to that."

"I hope you do," she purred.

"I'll see you in a few."

Cade hung up ready to get on the road. After Aaron and Abby took their seats in the car, the driver took off toward the hotel.

"Cade, are you even listening to me?" Abby asked.

His thoughts were on Callie and he didn't know she was speaking.

Aaron chimed in before he could respond.

"No, he's not listening to you. He's got one thing on his mind right now and it has nothing to do with work, press or promoting anything. You're wasting your breath. If I were you, I would wait two days and catch him up then."

"Just so that I'm clear, you really don't want to be disturbed until it's time for you to fly out to New York? Suppose it's an emergency?" Abby pleaded.

"The only emergency I want to know about is in regards to my brothers and my grandparents.

Everything else you can take care of or delegate to someone else and as long as no one disturbs me, everyone will keep their job at the end of my two day respite. As far as I'm concerned there is no other emergency that someone else can't attend to. I do want to talk to you about meals, etc. for the next two days in the suite."

"Before you finish that statement, it's already taken care of."

Cade looked at her puzzled, not sure he was understanding.

"Taken care of how?" he asked.

Abby leaned toward him and spoke as quietly as she could so that the driver could not hear them.

"Your guest has given me instructions for meals for the next two days and everything is taken care of."

Cade smiled.

"Got it. The subject is closed then because I'm sure my guest has it all planned out."

"That she does," Abby replied and leaned back.

They continued with idle chatter until the car pulled up to the hotel. Cade exited to a slew of press, not knowing how they knew he would be at the hotel. Thankfully they were not allowed inside. He exited his car and went inside straight to the elevator that would take him to his suite and shortly afterward, to Callie.

"How long do you think they'll hang around outside waiting for me to come out?" he asked

Aaron when they entered his suite.

"Not long. Abby is right now informing them that you would grant them a short interview in two days when you leave for New York. She is asking them to give you a break while you get a couple of days rest in the midst of the major promotional tour you're on. I'm sure they'll wait around a little while to see if she's telling the truth and then they'll go away, but return in two days."

"That's good. I'm glad Callie is already here and no one would see her coming it. She would have a heart attack if she thought someone saw her."

He wanted to question Cade about the hide and seek game they were playing. Since they were alone, it was a good time to inquire.

"Cade, what is the deal with so much privacy? You've been seen with women before and it's obvious you like Callie."

"This is all her, man. I told you the story of some things in her past about being linked to other entertainers and then having her name dragged through the mud about her being an opportunist. She's even lost a couple of jobs behind it and she doesn't want to go through that anymore. I agreed that I would protect her and her image because I really wanted to see her and spend some time with her. So far it's worked out good. I don't know how much of this I'm going to be able to stand. I already feel myself wanting to see her more and more and I don't know how many ways I can come up with to secretly see her. We both have our work lives and now that our personal lives are colliding, I don't want to hide her away like some secret affair. I really like her Aaron and I know she's feeling me too, but I can also respect her desire to be taken seriously in her career. I'm okay going along with this for now, but depending on where things go, she and I will probably have to talk about this subject again."

Aaron sympathized with his friend's dilemma and he would continue to do what he could to help.

"Are you ready for me to go get her yet?"

Cade looked at him like he had two heads.

"You mean you're still standing here and haven't left to get her yet?" he joked.

"I'm already gone," Aaron laughed while he left the room. "Call her and let her know I'm on my way to her suite."

Cade did that immediately.

"Hey you! Aaron is on his way to your suite."

"I'll see you in a few minutes then," Callie replied before hanging up.

Cade hung up the phone and started pacing like and expectant father. He surprised himself at the desperation he was feeling over the need to get her in his arms. They had only spent one night together and that one night wasn't nearly enough for him. She was already getting under his skin in a good way and definitely on his mind constantly.

To keep himself busy until she arrived, he

grabbed his luggage and took everything into the bedroom. He'd stayed at this hotel several times before and remembered the suite had a nice Jacuzzi. He was looking forward to taking advantage of it.

Before long, he heard Aaron call his name. He turned and went back into the main room and even though Aaron's six-foot five frame was massive compared to Callie, all he saw was her and she was even more beautiful than he remembered. She was standing looking at him in a sexy red dress which had to be made specifically for her. It complimented her assets and he couldn't wait to get his hands on said assets.

"Where do you want these?" Aaron asked.

It took Cade a few moments to notice Aaron was holding armfuls of bags.

"What is all that?"

"Ask Callie. They came along with her."

"I figured if you were going to keep me hostage for two days we should at least eat. That's food I asked Abby to order from your favorite restaurant and also some cheeses, fruits, wine and a few other things. Aaron, you can put them in the kitchen and I'll take care of everything after you leave."

Aaron noticed neither Callie nor Cade looked directly at him when they spoke. They never took their eyes off of each other.

"Okay, I'm going to sit everything down on the counter and hightail it out of here. The two of you look like you're ready to jump on each other whether I'm here or not."

"Man, I suggest you move swiftly. You may not want to be here for what's about to happen. This is about to be for the grown and sexy only," Cade warned, still never taking his eyes off of Callie standing before him looking delectable.

Aaron rushed and came back in the room, placing the card key to Cade's room on the entry table and opened the door to leave.

"See you in two day and try not to hurt him too much. He has a busy couple of weeks ahead him and we need him in one piece."

"I'll try my best, but I'm not making any promises," she added.

"Goodbye Aaron and remind Abby that I meant what I said when I told her no disturbance at all and that includes her."

"Got it. See you in two days."

17

They were finally alone after too much time apart. Before they got caught up in their reunion, he went to the door and placed the do not disturb sign on the opposite side so that hotel staff wouldn't interrupt them.

He then feasted his eyes on her.

"You look beautiful."

Callie smiled as she turned her head to the side to look up at him. Even in high-heeled shoes, he still towered over her with his six-foot four stance.

Neither of them waited another second as they met each other halfway and each tried to devour the other as what started out as a passionate kiss turned into a duel. Their tongues fought for control as their hands roamed all over each other as if they needed to verify that they were together again in person. The room was quiet except for their heavy breathing. As soon as one thought that the other was ready to pull away, the duel started over again. Cade licked while she sucked and then he nibbled lightly on her top lip while she nibbled on his bottom. They found a rhythm that worked and heightened their craving for each other.

"I would love to say let's take this slow and easy, but since we have two days, I'll reserve slow and easy for later," he said reaching into his pocket to retrieve a condom.

Not wasting any time, she fumbled with his zipper while he pulled her dress down over her shoulders and watched it fall to the floor.

"Oh my goodness!" he exclaimed when he saw what she had on underneath. "Are you trying to kill me? I'm so enthralled by it I'm thinking of not removing it from your body."

"Less talking, more sexing," Callie said while continuing to work his zipper.

"Whoa, carefully sweetheart."

She knew what that meant. She could see his hard as a rock shaft straining long and thick against his zipper and the last things she wanted to do was injure that magical part of him because she was too impatient to take her time. She could feel the heat of him pulsing against her hand as she worked to free him from the confines of his pants. Once she had his pants open, she lid them along with his boxer briefs to the floor. When she stood back up to her full height, Cade surprised her and lifted her off of her feet and into his arms and circled her legs around his back. If it wasn't for the barrier of her barely there panties, he would have slipped right into her. She wound her body a little, letting him know what she wanted and needed.

"I'm right there with you baby, but not yet," he replied knowing what she needed didn't need words; her body movements were enough.

He found her lips before she could open her mouth to complain, snapping them shut with a hard, demanding kiss. While her legs remained tight around his waist, he reached up and tangled his fingers into the fullness of her long wavy hair that was cascading around her shoulders and gripping her head, he pulled her even harder to his lips for an enduring kiss that included using his tongue to mate with hers in a kiss that was as old as time.

Callie rocked as Cade's penis pushed into her stomach while she continued to show him what she needed. To her he was taking too long because he wasn't even inside of her yet and she felt like she was about to shoot off like a rocket.

"Baby, I know what you need, but I want to taste you this time, something I didn't get to do before. It was all I could think about when I knew I would see you today."

He walked them slowly backwards until he reached the edge of the chaise lounge. He untangled her legs from around him and placed her on her back on the chair. When she went to close her legs, he shook his head no.

"Don't close yourself off from me. I want to see you just like this."

Cade reached up to remove his as his flesh stirred and twitched as if it were searching for her. When Callie licked her lips, the sight didn't escape him.

"We'll have time for that later," he crooned. "Right now, I'm a starving man."

She knew his intention and her body zinged in anticipation of what was to come.

He leaned down to remove her panties.

"I see these were made for easy removal," he said noticing the ties on each side of her hips. He pulled the strings and the panties fell away.

"I'm leaving the heels on. It's sexy as hell!" he exclaimed.

He ran his hands up both of her legs drawing sweet moans from her as he traveled up her body. His hands made their way across her taut stomach and up until he found the mounds of her breasts. He squeezed and tugged on the hard nipples and not being able to control himself, he leaned down and took first one and then the other into his mouth through the thin fabric. Callie's body lifted up off of the chair in amazement and he watched as her excitement went to another level.

"I can't wait," she said huskily.

"I can't either, but this will be worth the wait, baby."

He removed the bra that was keeping him from feeling and kneading her flesh. Once he had her naked except for the heels, he moved back down her body bringing his face in direct contact with her skin. He ran his face across her thighs and the stubble on his chin inflamed her body as he ran it up and down her sensitive skin.

Callie wasn't prepared for what came next. She never took her eyes off of him as his face slid further up her thighs and as he kissed his way to her center, she rocked into him welcoming him in. Cade accepted and went directly for her sweet spot. He spread her legs wide, pushing them up and over his shoulders. When his tongue reached out to greet the hard nub that was staring back at him, Callie was transformed into a euphoric state.

She felt as he first licked then probed as if he was a man at a feast. He didn't let up when she tried to slide away from him, not because she wasn't enjoying it, but because he knew she was already close to the edge.

"Don't hold back baby, you know what I want. You taste so sweet," he said before going back in for another taste. He went between licking, sucking and nibbling, driving her wild.

"I'm close," she moaned.

"I know baby, just let go. I got you," he groaned and continued his assault, licking up the essence that spilled from her body.

He knew the moment she came and when she

did, he still didn't let up. He held on to her legs and feasted harder and deeper when he felt her reach out and grip his head holding him in place. He wasn't planning on going anywhere, but he loved the feel of her guiding him to where she needed him. As she spiraled over the edge she screamed his name until her hands fell limp at her side and her body went pliant under him.

Cade let her legs fall from his shoulders as he finally opened up the condom packet and sheathed himself.

"You taste like everything in the world that I love all rolled up in you."

Callie was able to finally open her eyes after the mind-blowing orgasm she'd just experienced in time to see him drag his point into home plate by sticking his tongue out to lick around his lips making sure he captured every single delicious taste of her.

Now that he placed the condom on, he joined her on the chair once again spreading her legs preparing for his entry. As he poised himself, he watched as she smiled, ready for her next climb up the mountain of pleasure. As he began entering her, she closed her eyes basking in the pure pleasure of the feel of him.

"Look at me baby. I want you to look at me as I join our bodies. Look at me and know that this is only the beginning."

He pushed in slowly at first, loving the feel of her

gripping him with her inner muscles. He had to grit his teeth to keep from having a premature release much quicker than he wanted. Her body gripped him tightly, milking and coaxing him to go deeper.

"I feel so full," Callie sighed into his ear.

"Me too baby. Hold on because this ride is about to get rocky."

She grabbed onto his shoulders and kept her gaze on his eyes and while he never took his from hers, she felt his lower body artfully move in and out of hers drawing out the pleasure for them.

Cade increased the pressure for even more enjoyment and as he did, he heard her breath quicken as he knew she was again about to crest and this time, he was right with her in her quest to reach that peak. Only then did he take his gaze from off of her because what slammed into him drew him back. In an animalistic response to what his body was experiencing, he howled as the force of his release, triggered by hers, forced him to pound into her like a wild man, uninhibited and out of control. Again and again, wave after wave of pleasure crashed over as Callie squealed with delight as she thrashed around like a she-devil.

Just when he thought her body was about to quiet down, it hummed to life under him again as a second wave of pleasure hit her and she went over the edge a second time. Her second orgasm triggered another for him and to his delight and amazement, he welcomed it as he clenched his jaw and thrust into her body again and again as his strokes became swifter. His second climax was longer and more powerful than the first. It went on and on until finally he shuddered through the last of his spasms and collapsed on top of Callie who was slowly coming around now that her body was calming.

They neared exhaustion, to the point that neither could move. Cade was concerned that his weight would crush her and attempted to move from on top of her, but she pulled him back down.

"Don't move. I love the feel of you still inside of me. This feels perfect."

Cade agreed and though he stayed on top of her, he leaned his weight on his arms, laid his head on her chest and closed his eyes. The world around him rocked like never before and if he recovered, he knew he was in trouble. Nothing like what he just experienced had ever happened to him before and knew that it only would again with her. He knew he was falling for her and he was falling hard.

**

"Eventually we're going to have to get up from this chair and find the bed."

Callie kept her arms around Cade's neck as he continued to hold her tightly on his lap. With his head resting on her chest, he leaned his head down further and grasped one of her nipples between his teeth and tugged lightly giving it caresses with his tongue. It was obvious to her that he had no plans of moving.

"I don't know if I can move any part of my body other than my tongue right now and as you can feel, it's kind of busy."

She could feel it alright and every tug from his teeth sent a surge through her body right to the core of her. They were still intimately connected and she could feel his flesh as it began hardening inside of her.

"I feel another part of you that's coming to life right now and before it does, you're going to be uncomfortable in this position soon."

Cade released her nipple with a popping sound and raised his head to look up at her.

"You have a glow about you that amazes me when I look at you. You are so damn lovely."

She kissed him on the lips.

"The glow you see is the look of a woman who has just experienced two very powerful orgasms and surprised that she's still awake. I know you flipped us over so that I would be on your lap, thinking it would be more comfortable, but it's not on this little chair. Let's get up and eat."

"I don't want to leave the warmth of your body even though I'm starving," he murmured.

"There is plenty of food, but you have to untangle yourself from my body so that I can fix us something."

Cade slid back on the chair and helped her lift

up. She felt the emptiness the minute they were no longer joined. She stood for a minute without moving letting her legs get use to her now being on them.

He noticed she looked unstable.

"You need some help getting to the room? You look a little shaky."

"You would too with the workout you just gave my body. I should probably put something on and so should you before we end up right back where we just were. This sexual palette of yours is maddening!" she quipped.

"I must say, you keep up with me quite nicely," he said walking toward her.

Callie put her hand out to stop him.

"Oh, no you don't. Food first before you pass out. Where are my clothes?"

"I don't know, but the bra and panties I took off of you, I'm going to need to see that again on you and the next time, I promise to take my time and enjoy seeing you in it. This time I had built up such a need for you that even though I could see that it was sexy as hell, I was more interested in getting to what it covered."

Callie smiled knowing exactly how he felt. This was going to be a fun two days of catching up on time they missed apart from each other.

18

"Angel, we're in the middle of taping so I can't talk long. Is something wrong?"

Callie finally had to answer her phone since Angel had called three times in a row and she didn't know if it was an emergency.

"You're so busy working I'm sure you haven't seen the latest Hollywood news. I know you mentioned to me that Cade was in Morocco, but you didn't tell me about the princess he has been linked to for years. There are pictures of them splattered all over the channels and newspapers. Did you see them?"

She had no idea what Angel was talking about. Cade was in Morocco, but she knew nothing about a princess.

"Angel what are you talking about."

"Hang up from me and then go on line to any website and you'll see what I'm talking about. Do it now," she shouted and then hung up in Callie's ear.

She took her phone and went to a quiet spot off the set. She logged onto a popular site that frequently broadcasted the latest in entertainment. What she saw caused an ache in her chest. Cade was hugged up on a beautiful woman and the caption said something about the woman and Cade rekindling a romance everyone thought was dead. It appears they had been seen together in cozy situations for the past few days.

Ever since the two days she'd spent with him a few weeks ago, they had talked frequently, sometimes several times a day. A week ago, he had to take a trip to Morocco for some star-studded event and she had not heard from him since nor had he returned to the states. She quickly scanned the article that questioned how long Cade would stay with the princess and whether they were once again an item. She read on when the same story gave some of the history between them.

It seems a few years back, they were inseparable appearing at functions together and there were also photos of them kissing, holding hands and cuddling. Not wanting to read anymore, she shut off her phone and stood still to gather herself as jealousy like she's never experienced before made her chest ache. Had Cade really been seeing this woman while he was away from her? They had an understanding that though she knew he had to keep his image up for publicity sake, he wouldn't get intimately involved with anyone and she agreed to the same. It looks like Cade didn't keep up his end of the deal. The photos taken were definitely intimate looking.

As she returned to the set where a scene was about to be taped, others had seen the stories as well and tongues began wagging with stories of Cade's prowess with women. She couldn't find anyone who wasn't talking about it and she was already tired of hearing it. She excused herself to find a quiet place where there was no gossip for her to hear. She turned her phone back on and sent Angel a text that she saw the story, didn't want to talk about it and that she was fine. Angel sent her a text back offering to be an ear if she wanted to talk. At the moment, she didn't want anything other than a call from Cade letting her know what was going on.

**

Cade got back to the villa he'd been staying in while in Morocco and was concerned of what Callie was thinking back in Los Angeles once she got a whiff of the entertainment headlines about him.

"Call her man," Aaron said coming into the room, joining him.

"I want to, but I'm not sure how effective I will be on the phone trying to explain everything to her. Princess Galia and I have a past and it doesn't matter that nothing is going on now, the press will spin it as if there is."

"So you and the princess didn't reconnect and nothing happened?"

Aaron had just arrived in Morocco to take over the security detail sending Sean home for a few days. He didn't know what had been going on.

"No, nothing happened other than a few photo opportunities. It's all for the camera and nothing else. She's trying to launch an acting career and you know all press is good press and linking her back to me would get tongues wagging."

Aaron smiled.

"What are you smiling about?" he asked.

"Bro, there was a time when you didn't care who you were photographed with doing whatever. It never bothered you, but now, look at you, your first concern is about Callie."

Aaron was right. The moment he got a look at some of the press, he realized what he thought was innocent acting for the camera looked suspect and he worried about what Callie must be thinking.

"Man, I've fallen so hard and fast for her it still shocks me. Not that she isn't worthy of my fall from being the player because she is. I think about her all the time and now I even think about her when I'm making career decisions. I can't play things down for the media because this is who I am to them and remember, to the world I'm not seeing anyone so it's normal for me to be seen like what's in these news stories. Callie won't consider letting anyone in on the fact that we're involved for fear of what it would do to her reputation. I'm stuck between a rock and a hard place trying to figure out how to carry this and not do anything to jeopardize my relationship with her."

"Cade, like I said, just call her and explain at least until you get home. If she cares about you as much as I know you care about her, and I'm sure she does, I think she'll understand. The longer you wait to call her, the more she'll think you have something to hide."

"You're right. I need to talk to her."

"Listen, if you're cool and you plan to hang around here for a while, I'm going to go get something to eat and check-in to my room. Handle your business and if you need me before I get back here, call."

"Thanks."

Now that he was alone, Cade relaxed and pulled out his phone to call Callie.

"Hi," Callie said somberly into the phone.

Cade knew she would be upset.

"None of its true Callie. Not one word of what you may be reading is true." He paused. "Wait, some of it is. I was intimately involved with her a few years ago, but not since then and definitely not now."

His explanation was met with silence.

"I saw the pictures and the two of you look cozy."

"Come on Callie, you know there are some things I have to do for the camera and this is one of those things. She's launching an acting career and my being with her is only about publicity and nothing else. We wouldn't have to worry about any of this if we could stop hiding out at my house and in hotels sneaking around like two teenagers all to protect your image. Haven't we been seeing each other long enough that you know I'm not interested in anyone else?"

"It's not about that. You're doing what you are accustomed to doing and that's being Cade Weston. I can only go by what I see and what I see right now is a very beautiful woman draped over you like you're hers. I know I have no right to be jealous, but I am."

"Baby, there is no need for jealousy. I'm all yours and I'm not tempted by anyone. You have to trust me, especially when we're thousands of miles apart like now."

"I do trust you Cade, but it's hard for me to separate Cade from heartthrob".

He was disappointed that she called him that. He didn't mind hearing it from others, but he never wanted to hear it from her. It gave meaning to the womanizer he used to be and vilified who he had become since getting involved with her.

"Don't do that Callie. Don't call me that because that's not who I am. I can be that for you, but not for anyone else and not in the way that everyone else uses it. You've set the rules of our relationship and I've gone along with it. You have to believe me when I say that no matter what the media writes about, there is nothing there. Can you give me some credit for all that I have been doing to make sure my professional life doesn't get in the way of our personal life? I'm trying to do things your way and I still have to be me and that me is still Cade Weston."

He waited for her response and was again met with silence.

"We are too far away from each other to let this cause a problem. I have a job to do and the next leg of that job is taking me to China tomorrow. Can we talk about this when I get back to the states?"

Callie heard the subdued tone of his voice and she felt bad. She didn't want to make him feel bad for being who he is expected to be. He was right that she did set all the rules for their relationship and she had no right to be upset because he's being him. She shook off her doubt and dropped the weight of what she read. She knew first-hand how the media can turn a story several different ways with all of them being unflattering.

"Baby, I'm sorry if I'm making you feel like you have to plead your case with me. I do trust you. I admit I was a little upset when I first saw the story and read the headlines, but you're right. I have to let you be you and accept the fact that this is part of what you do as Cade Weston and I'm okay with that. It's not that I don't trust you; it's all about jealousy which was my first reaction."

Cade relaxed and exhaled the breath he was holding. He didn't want anything to come between them, especially some entertainment news story made up to sell stories and hype images.

"I'll be in China for a week and then I'm flying home. Since I've been gone for several weeks, I think we need some down time to reconnect. Dinner at my house when I return?"

Callie smiled though he couldn't see it.

"Dinner sounds perfect," she replied happily.

"I hate being away from you for these long stretches of time. I need to see you, kiss you, touch you and especially taste you."

The word taste made her sex jump at the thought of his expertise at tasting her.

"I know. I miss you. How busy are you going to be in a few hours?" she asked with a hint of seduction in her voice.

Cade caught on to something naughty in her voice and he was all in.

"Give me a few hours and let's face chat. I have something to show you," she said.

Cade growled, liking the sound of where she was going with this.

"Baby, I will be ready with bells on."

She laughed.

"Bells are okay, but make sure you're not wearing anything else."

"I will if you will," he quickly countered.

"I'll see you in a few hours then and thanks for

calling. I was feeling down, but not anymore. Do you and I'll stop reading the entertainment news."

"I miss you baby. I'll see you in a few hours. Send me a text when you're ready. I'm ready now and I would show you, but I'll hold on to that until later."

19

Cade felt apprehensive which was a feeling that wasn't common for him. He stood before crowds of thousands, acted on camera and spoke with no trace of nervousness, but hearing that Callie wasn't on the set because she was ill put him on edge. He didn't want anyone to notice his uneasiness and with the crowd around him throwing a million questions at him at one time about one thing or the other regarding the show, he was hearing none of it. His only thought was to remove himself, find a quiet spot away from ears that would be listening so that he could check in on her.

He looked for Aaron and gave his signal which meant it was time for him to get rid of the distractions. As Aaron and another member of the security team dispersed everyone around him, he slipped off to his private office and called Callie to be sure she was okay.

The first time he called, his call went to her

voicemail, but because he was determined to find out how she was feeling, he called several more times until she finally answered.

He could tell from the sound of her voice that she must really be under the weather.

"Callie? Are you alright? I got here to the set for today's taping and I didn't see you. I heard others say you wouldn't be here today because you're sick."

He didn't get a response other than a slight grunt.

"Callie, did you hear me? Baby, I need you to answer me? What's wrong?"

"I have the flu or something. I'm hot and cold at the same time, I'm sure I have a fever and my whole body aches. I tried to make it to the set today, but I couldn't get out of bed. Every time I tried, I felt dizzy. I'll be there tomorrow for sure. I don't know what happened because I didn't feel this way yesterday. It just crept up on me sometime in the night and this morning, I couldn't shake it."

He heard her muffled words and knowing the person she was, he had no doubt she tried to make it to work and only pain would keep her from it.

"What can I do for you?" he asked with concern.

"I'll be okay. I'm going to order some soup from room service in a little while and I'll be as good as new."

"Baby, from the sound of your voice, I think you'll need more than soup. Have you taken anything or seen a doctor?"

He heard her attempt to laugh through a serious coughing spell.

"It's the flue and it's common. Not everything needs a doctor, but I did take some over the counter medicine and I'll be fine."

"I'm coming to check on you to be sure you're okay. I don't like how you sound."

Callie knew if she didn't perk up, he would be on his way and she knew he had a busy day on set."

"You will do no such thing," she said trying to sound more awake and more like her usual self.

"I can't leave you there by yourself when I know you're sick. Let me come and at least bring you something to eat."

"The hotel has a great kitchen staff and they can bring me whatever I need. Don't fuss over me because I'll be fine in a few hours and you have a lot to do on set for today's taping. You can't disappear without it being noticed and I don't want people to start talking. Who knows what they'll think with me being out today and all of a sudden you're out too."

Cade knew that Callie was always on guard about someone discovering that they've been seeing each other. She purposely avoided any contact with him that seemed out of the ordinary for a member of the production staff who may be looking on. He hated that they had to disconnect in public while his feelings for her grew stronger daily. He tried, but couldn't figure out a way to get around her resistance and so he went along with her plan to keep what they share from everyone.

Now that she was ill, he wanted to put her reservations aside and take care of her.

"Callie, I'm going to have Maria come to you and help you put some things together and I'll have Aaron and Sean pick you up and bring you out to my house. I can't stand the idea of you being in that hotel by yourself and you're sick. This way they can look after you and get you back up and moving around quicker."

"You will do no such thing. I'm fine here by myself and it's just the flu which I'm sure will work itself out in a day or two. All I need is some rest. Continue with your work today and don't say you don't have any because I know what's on your schedule. I promise I will call you later to let you know how I'm doing and I bet by then, I'll be up and moving around."

"Cade, you're needed on the set." He turned toward his office door when one of the production assistants came to get him.

"See, I knew you had a busy day. I need to go back to sleep anyway. I was up most of the night and sleep feels real good about now. Why don't you call me when you get some free time and I promise you I'll be feeling better? Hearing your voice has made an improvement already."

He didn't believe her, but he had no choice. They were already a few days behind due to set reconstruction and he wanted to get a few episodes of season two done while season one was a few months away from premiering.

"Okay baby, but keep your phone right by you and if you don't answer when I call, I'm coming to check on you in person and I don't care who knows about it."

"I'll keep it right here on the other pillow where I know you'd be if you were here with me."

"Get some sleep and I'll call you in a few hours."

Cade hung up after his assistant again called out to him. He tried to put aside his concern for Callie so that he could focus on the show. He stood, shook off the worry and reached for the door. Before he opened it, he stiffened knowing he wouldn't be able to concentrate knowing she was alone. He opened the door and asked Aaron to step inside.

"What's up boss man, you good?" Aaron asked.

"Callie isn't feeling good. According to her she has the flu or something and after I spoke with her a few minutes ago, I don't like the fact that she's at her hotel by herself. I can't leave the set to check on her and I need to know that she's okay."

"You want me to go check on her for you?"

"Actually, what I want is for you to stop at my house, pick up Maria and take her to the hotel to pack a few of Callie's things and bring her to the house. Connie and Maria can look after her and make sure she's eating and not getting worse. I know she's stubborn, but don't leave that hotel without her even if you have to pick her up and carry her out," he said sternly.

Aaron smiled and Cade shook his head.

"Do I have to say it?"

"Say it and die brother!" Cade bellowed, laughing at himself.

"Are you going to deny you're falling in love with her?"

"I'm not admitting or denying anything and the longer we stand here, the longer Callie is at that hotel by herself. I'm going to call Maria and tell her to expect you. I also need to explain to her who Callie is and what I need her to do."

"Man, I'm so proud of how you've grown!" Aaron quipped, lightening the mood.

"I'm doing what any man should do when a woman he's involved with is sick."

"Yeah well, this isn't the Cade I've known all these years who keeps women at arms-length. You've never allowed a woman you're intimately involved with to step one foot into that house since you built it a few years ago claiming it was your place of solitude. Do you even realize how easily you've allowed her to get closer to you than any other woman ever has? I told you when you found that woman, your whole life would change."

He didn't try to deny what he was feeling for Callie and since Aaron was not only his friend, but the keeper of his secrets, he didn't know a reason to not share his true feelings.

"I'm falling in love with her and I've never been happier than I am when I'm with her."

"Why are you keeping the fact that you're seeing each other a big secret? The lengths you are going to keep this a secret are crazy, especially when you know what you feel for her is genuine."

Cade didn't know either other than it's what she wanted.

"The secrecy isn't my doing; it's Callie's. She wants to be taken seriously in the entertainment business and due to some past issues, she doesn't want the media portraying her as a groupie getting ahead because she's with me. I agreed to keep our relationship a secret to respect her privacy and her wishes, but I hate it. I don't care what the media says or does because unless a story comes from me, it's all gossip anyway."

"Now I'm really shocked! For the past few weeks since the two of you have been seeing each other, I thought you were behind all the clandestineness I've had to endure making sure everyone was blind to your relationship and all along it's been Callie's idea. It's sad that she feels she has to do that to be taken seriously. That woman has a lot of talent."

"She's not like any other woman and for once, I would have no problem letting everyone see that we're a couple. If I didn't agree to it, she was ready to walk away from me. I don't know where things are going with us, but I do know that I'll get nothing done today if I don't know that she's okay."

Not giving it much more thought, he reached for his phone and dialed the private line at his house and Maria answered on the first ring.

"Maria, I need a huge favor. Aaron is going to stop by the house and pick you up in about an hour. I have someone who's going to be staying with us for a few days and she's a little under the weather with the flu. Right now she's staying at a hotel in Los Angeles and I need you to go with Aaron to pack up a few days' worth of clothing and essentials and bring her back to the house."

"Which one of the guest rooms would you like me to set her up in?" Maria asked.

Cade hesitated knowing his response would come as a shock to her. He didn't have a choice because he wanted her close.

"You can make her comfortable in my room and get her whatever she needs. Have Connie make some of her award winning chicken noddle soup and make sure she's comfortable. I know I wasn't planning to be at the house for the next week, but I'll be home later tonight. Now, she may push back on leaving the hotel, but don't leave without her."

"I see, Mr. Cade. This is a special woman to you?"

"Yes, Maria. She is very special to me."

"Well it's about time someone special has entered our lives. Connie and I will take very good care of her so don't you worry about anything. Tell

Aaron I'll need him to stop at the store so that I can pick up your favorites since you'll be here this week. Give him a list of anything special you want me to pick up or that you want Connie to make and I'll be ready to go when he gets here. Tell him I said not to be late because your lady is waiting."

Cade laughed knowing Callie was about to be taken care of better than he was. Maria and Connie were life family and both had been taking care of him for years.

"He won't be late and in fact, he's leaving right now while I'm talking to you."

He looked at Aaron who got the clue and headed to the door.

"Take Sean with you and as always, thanks man."

Aaron gave the thumbs up and left.

After giving some last minute instructions to Maria, he hung up and a weight lifted. He hoped Callie wouldn't fight too much when Aaron showed up at the hotel with Maria. It was either that or he'd have to find a way to stay with her at the hotel without the world knowing about it and he doubted if he would be able to do it. This way, he knew she would be taken care of and he wouldn't have to worry about her while he continued with his busy schedule of appearances.

20

In the distance, Callie could hear someone knocking on her door. She was in and out of sleep, but whoever it was didn't mind being persistent. She had a feeling that unless she got up to answer it, they weren't going away.

"I'm coming!" she hollered.

She slipped first one leg and then the other out from under the comforter and sat on the edge of the bed waiting to see if she would once again feel lightheaded as she did when she tried to get up earlier. Feeling okay, she slowly stood and though she swayed a little, found her footing and walked to the door. She peeped and saw the face of Aaron smiling back at her through the peephole and quickly opened it.

"Aaron, tell Cade I'm going to kill him. Where is he?" she said looking out into the hallway beyond him. She didn't see him, but she did see a woman she didn't know.

"He's not with me. He sent me to get you to take you to his house. He's worried about you being here at the hotel alone and you're ill."

He then turned to Maria.

"This is Maria and she's the woman who has had the responsibility of taking good care of Cade for the past ten years. She's going to help you get some things packed and she and Connie are going to look after you for a few days."

He saw her about to fuss and cut her off.

"Don't try it. You know if he sent me, he means business and believe me when I tell you, it's not Cade you would have to deal with if you don't come along. Maria here is not to be played with and what Cade asks her to do, she does and nothing stops her, not even a stubborn woman, so turn around, get dressed and I'll have a seat while the two of you get what you need."

Before she could say a word, Maria said hello and Callie stood still as the stranger reached up to feel her head to check her temperature.

"You're burning up child. You shouldn't be in this hotel by yourself with what is clearly a high fever. Let's get you dressed and out of here so that I can look after you properly."

Maria didn't wait for an answer as she took Callie by the hand and walked her toward the bedroom of the suite. Callie looked back at Aaron for support and he looked away as if to say he would have no parts of her trying to get out of leaving with them. She turned back around and followed along with Maria when Aaron waved her on as he sat back and relaxed in the chair near the door.

"Why don't you get dressed while I put some things in a suitcase for you. Is your suitcase in the closet here?"

"Yes it is and I can pack my things. I don't want you to have to wait on me."

"Nonsense Ms. Callie. Do you need help getting dressed? You look a little weak and light on your feet."

Callie turned her head from left to right as she watched Maria zip around the room gathering things. It looked like she was a pro at this and Callie assumed she wasn't the first damsel in distress that she's had to rescue for Cade. The thought made her a little uneasy, but felling ill, she wasn't up for a fight to stay where she was. She grabbed a few things from the dresser and went into the bathroom to shower and change.

During her shower, she wondered if she was making the right move going to Cade's house. They were spending more time together and she was definitely falling hard for him, but opening up their relationship to others, including the staff at his house was risky. Questions flooded her mind. Why was she taking such a risk knowing what has happened to her in the past? Not only was she putting her feelings on the line, but her career as well. Was the time spent with him worth the risk? She fought hard to get to where she was and she didn't want to see it crumble because she's fallen for the sexiest man alive and there is a chance he's simply enjoying their time together.

**

Maria exited the car first once they had arrived at the house and Sean drove into the garage and lowered the door. She proceeded quietly so that she wouldn't waken a still sleeping Callie who had nodded off the minute they were seated in the car.

While Sean exited the car and went around to the back to get Callie's bags, Maria went to the callbox on the wall to call for Connie.

"Connie, we're here."

Immediately the door to the house opened and Connie exited.

"How is she?" she asked as they all looked into the car to see if she had moved.

"She has a high fever and according to Mr. Cade she has the flu. I'll have Aaron pick her up and carry her to Mr. Cade's room so that we don't wake her up. I think she hasn't been able to get much sleep," Maria said.

"I've put clean linens on the bed and the soup is done whenever she's ready to eat."

"Thanks Connie. I stopped and picked up some cold medicine at the store and a few other things Mr. Cade asked me to get. We can get those bags while Sean brings in her luggage. Let's get her into bed. And resting comfortably and I'll let Mr. Cade know she's here and we're taking good care of her."

**

Cade left the set as soon as he saw Aaron return after picking up Callie and dropping her off at the house.

"How was she when you left and before you answer, the next time I call you, in order to keep our friendship intact, I suggest you answer the phone," he said jokingly to keep the conversation light, but Aaron knew he was serious.

"I would have answered, but you kept calling every five minutes. Callie still has the flu and she's still sick. When I left the house she was in your bed sleeping comfortably with Connie and Maria hovering over her like mother hens."

"I wanted to be sure she didn't put up too much of a fuss after you arrived at her hotel room demanding she leave or else. I know Maria gave her that speech didn't she?"

"You know her well. There was no way Callie was going to be able to stay at that hotel once Maria arrived. She walked in the door packing stuff up and ushering her around. She even had me carry her up to your room because she didn't want to wake her."

Cade's concern lessened knowing Maria and Connie would do everything to make her feel better especially if it made him happy.

"I do need to warn you about something," Aaron

said.

"What?"

"Maria and Connie are running around like it's Christmas day. They're excited and they want to know more so be ready to give them the rundown on how you've fallen in love."

Cade started to contradict him when he was cut off.

"Save it brother. You may not want to tell me, but I already know. You're in love and I'm happy for you. Now you need to tell Callie and the two of you need to work out this relationship thing."

He exhaled and didn't put up a fight. Aaron, was right; he was in love.

**

Cade walked into his house and was about to head to his room to check on Callie when Maria came up to him.

"She's sleeping Mr. Cade so don't go up to your room and wake her up. She's had a sleepless evening and now I think she's finally sleeping peacefully."

"Did she eat anything?" he asked.

"She ate a little of the soup Connie made. She's been drinking a lot of water and some juice. I picked up plenty of flu medicine at the store and she took two pills about an hour ago."

He was relieved knowing he didn't have to worry.

"I like her Mr. Cade. I didn't get a chance to talk

to her a whole lot, but my first instinct tells me she's a beautiful woman and not just on the outside. I hope you are realizing that."

"Maria, I realized that the moment I met her. You have to know she's different because I've never brought a woman I'm involved with to this house in the five years that I've lived here."

She smiled and he recognized the silly smile as the same one that Aaron sports whenever they talk about Callie. Everyone seems to think she is the one for him.

Connie walked up while they were talking and he noticed the same silly smile as Maria. He could do or say anything but smile and shake his head at the two mother figures.

"The two of you are happy there's a woman around?" he asked.

"We're happy if this means you're learning to finally settle down with someone. We don't like to see all the women you parade around for the cameras and all the stories written about you and all those women. It's time for something more serious and I think our prayers have been answered," Connie added.

"What prayers?"

"Prayers that you would one day recognize you are worthy of love and not just one night stands."

They walked away while he stood still, pondering their words. He turned in the direction of the stairs and took them two at a time to get to the woman he loved. As he climbed, he thought of the nickname, heartthrob that was given to him and it now held a new meaning because his heart began throbbing in his chest as he got closer to seeing Callie and having her in his arms once again, sick or not.

21

Callie woke feeling a little dizzy, but she could tell her fever had gone down thanks to the care she was getting from Maria and Connie. She was on her third day at Cade's house and according to him, two of the days she'd pretty much slept through. She was beginning to feel more like herself though small traces of being sick still lingered. Cade's staff were lifesavers as they brought her medicine and soup and made sure she kept fluids in. Now that she was feeling better, it was time for her to get back to her own place. She turned to sit up on the edge of the bed and was greeted by Cade's deep, velvety voice.

"Don't think about getting out of this bed today unless it's to go to the bathroom and then right back to this bed," she heard him say. When she looked over at him, he spoke without ever opening his eyes.

The sight of him had her mind going back to the

times that they'd made love and she wanted him even now as he lay there looking like a bronzed god.

"Cade you should not be in bed this close to me."

"I've been in this bed with you for the past three nights even though you slept through most of it and the worst part of it should be over so I think I'm good if I haven't gotten sick yet. I wasn't sleeping in a separate bed from you. It felt good holding you in my arms all night long these past few days without having to get up and rush off anywhere. I can't remember the last time I've spent this many nights in a row at this house."

"Don't you have a full day of press today about the new recording artist you signed last week? I remember us talking about the big day. What time is it anyway? You're going to be late."

He didn't move and still had not opened his eyes.

"I don't care what time it is or what's on my calendar. Believe me, in a few short minutes Abby will begin lighting up every phone in order to reach me about what's on my schedule for today. That press conference isn't until later in the day and anything else I had scheduled for earlier than that will be canceled. I plan to stay right here for most of the morning. I never get to relax and lay around and I'm going to use the fact that you're sick to tell everyone to cut me some slack today."

A nervous, uncomfortable feeling settled over her as he said everyone. She wondered outside of

Aaron, Sean, Abby, Maria and Connie, who else had he told about them.

Cade opened his eyes when he felt her stiffen under his grasp.

"What's the matter Callie?"

"Who is everyone? You said you would tell everyone to cut you some slack. Who else knows about us?"

"Keep your panties on Callie; I only meant the same ones that you already know about and I was mainly speaking of Abby. Would it really be that bad if other people found out about us? It's a relationship and people have them every day."

"People don't have them every day with Cade Weston so don't toss this out like it's a regular thing. I'm not ready for people to know yet. I had to swear my parents to secrecy that they wouldn't tell anyone and Angel knows better. She knows I'd kill her if she let it slip to anyone. I haven't told anyone else and I hope you haven't told anyone outside of the small group who already knows."

He turned toward her.

"You are the first woman in the history of the world who doesn't want to be seen with me," he joked.

"It's not that I don't want to be seen with you; I don't want to be seen."

"What is so wrong with being seen? You're concerned because once everyone finds out we're an item your life will be open to scrutiny including bringing up what has happened to you in the past, something you should stop caring about. You know who you are, your family and friends know who you are and clearly I do, so why are you worried what others will think and by others I'm speaking about people who don't matter anyway."

She didn't respond, but leaned back and crawled back into bed facing him.

"Come here," he coaxed and she slipped into his embrace. He leaned down, kissed her on the lips and laughed as she attempted to push him away.

"Don't kiss me. You're going to get sick."

"I don't care. What I do care about is you, very much. I don't like that I have to hide you from the world as if I'm not proud to call you my lady. I want to be able to take you to events and go out on dates and not worry if a camera is capturing our every move. I want you to feel comfortable being with me without worry about someone saying you're doing so in order to get ahead. You trust your talent, I trust your talent, those around you trust your talent and that's all that matters. We can't keep this up forever Callie and you know that. Something has to give."

She shrugged knowing he spoke the truth.

"I hear you and I know that I'm being overly sensitive and too cautious, I got that. Can you give me a little more time? I think this arrangement is working out well and a huge plus is all of the time I get you to myself. I haven't told you this, but I'm meeting with some people next week about launching my clothing line."

Cade jumped with excitement and planted kisses across her face.

"I'm happy to hear you're finally pushing toward your dream? Is there anything I can do to help?"

"No, I want to do this on my own. One of the reasons why I wanted to wait before the world knows we're a couple is that I want to do this myself, making my own connections and making it happen because I did it and not because I'm Cade Weston's girlfriend."

Cade looked at her with a humorous look of shock and pretended to grab his chest as if he were having a heart attack.

"Wait, are you my girlfriend? Does that mean I'm your boyfriend? I must be doing something right," he jested.

Callie pinched his bare chest making him flinch in laughter.

"Okay, okay. I understand and again I'll leave it alone."

"Good, now I need to get home."

Cade held onto her.

"I'm serious. You're not going anywhere. I can tell you still have a slight fever though you sound a lot better than you did a few days ago. Just stay here and relax for the day. I have a crazy schedule so I won't be around to get on your nerves worrying about you. Connie and Maria will get you back to one hundred percent. They have nursed me back to health on many occasions."

"I can't stay here in this bed all day. What if someone comes by?"

Cade was losing patience.

"Stop it Callie. No one has come by here the last three days that you've been here and I've coming here every night. No one is going to come by, especially not unexpected and you really need to get over this. I can't help who I am so stop making me feel bad about being Cade Weston. I'm trying to make this work and you constantly push back as if this relationship is vile or disdain. So what if someone finds out about us? Would that really be so bad?" he asked.

Now she felt horrible.

"I'm sorry Cade. I'll stop."

He smiled the hundred watt smile she loved seeing on his handsome face and welcomed him when he leaned in for a sweet kiss. Before long, the kiss that started out as sweet and tender turned into one filled with hunger and longing.

She went into his arms as he pulled her closer, rolling them so that she now lay on top of his strong muscled chest.

"I told you, you're going to get sick kissing me like this."

"Don't ask me to stop," he said grinding up into her so that she could feel his pulsating flesh as it grew longer and thicker against her stomach.

Feeling him hard, hot and ready for her wreaked havoc on her senses and torture to her body.

"You're so hard," she whimpered.

"Something only you do to me."

No thoughts other than him floated mindlessly through her head as she reached down between them and slipped her hand inside of his pajama bottoms. She grabbed that part of him that time and again had brought her pleasure and stroked him from base to tip. When he groaned into her mouth, she increased the pace and pressure of her caress.

"Callie," Cade sighed, consumed by her attention to his hardening flesh.

"Shhh. Just enjoy baby."

Callie intensified the kiss by taking total control. She sought out his tongue and danced with it mimicking the way his body often entered hers bringing her pleasure beyond anything she'd ever experienced. She licked across the seam of his lips from one end to the other, adding in little nips along the way. She felt the straps of her top sliding down her shoulders and exhaled in relief as he took one nipple and suckled it while grabbing her hips to slide her across his heated flesh. The friction almost caused her to explode and they weren't intimately connected.

She regained her senses and took back control. He had always been the one to lead their encounters making sure his first priority was pleasuring her, but this time she wanted to please him. She removed his hands from her hips and placed them above his head. When he tried to move them back to her body, she pushed them back and looked into his eyes.

"Lay back and enjoy," she whispered.

Cade saw a determined looked in Callie's eyes and let her have her way. Sick or not, they couldn't resist each other and his body was too hot for her to deny her anything.

Callie smiled, feeling rejuvenated when Cade relaxed under her and allowed her full control over him. After placing a sweet kiss on his lips, she slid down and placed kisses across his jaw, his neck and spent a little extra time kissing and sucking on his chest. The act got a sensual reaction from him as he moaned and gyrated the lower part of his body, letting her know he loved what she was doing to him.

She didn't stop there as she went even further licking across his abs and his taut stomach, that visions of the ultimate man of every woman's dreams were made of. As she traveled further, she encountered the top of the hair that covered that part of him that brought her to her peak over and over again. Sliding down even further, she pulled his pajama bottoms down until they were completely off of his body and staring her in the face was his massive, turgid arousal. Her mouth watered at the thought of pleasing him this way for the first time. She'd wanted to do it on numerous occasions, but she suppressed her inner freak and held off until the time was right.

After taking in the incredible view of him, she watched his face as she opened her mouth and licked across the thick mushroomed head of him. The delight she saw on his face encouraged her to go further. As she ever so slowly took more of his rock hard member into her mouth, she watched his hazel eyes darken to a dark caramel brown color right before he closed them and threw his head back in need.

She took as much of him as she could get in and used her tongue to caress up and down the side of him before nuzzling him with her face, loving the hot touch of his flesh on her skin. She was about to take him in again when she felt him reach down and pulled her up, flush against him.

"Your mouth is incredible, but I think I'm going to explode in flames if I don't get inside of you."

She loved the sound of that and before she could utter a response, she helped him as he removed her thin pajama bottoms tossing them to the floor followed by her top that was dangling around her middle. She watched with glazed over eyes as he reached into the night stand, withdrew a condom and quickly donned it before lifting her up with poise, directly over his thick, throbbing shaft. She luxuriated in the feel as he pulsed while entering her body.

"I can roll you over if you don't have the energy from being sick."

"Right now I have the energy to run the races with the bulls. I need this," she said right before she began moving on him.

Cade tried to guide her movement to slow her down afraid that the tight grip she had on him would cause their lovemaking to end quicker than he wanted. Her body, humming with torrents of pleasure above him, forced a deep guttural, uncontrollable moan from him which threatened to shatter his sanity.

"Mine," he shouted.

Callie rolled her hips and when her body couldn't hold off any longer, she bucked and a dam of sexual pleasure overtook her actions and emotions and she let go. She rode up and down on him drawing every ounce of pleasure from him and equally giving the same.

"That's it baby," Cade groaned over and over.

Callie looked like a goddess coming apart on him and no longer feeling the need to drag his pleasure out any longer, he rocked his hips up and surged into her as his own pleasure slammed into him with the force of a tidal wave. Her small cries of delight continued to fuel his body as a flash of light exploded in his head, as his body now satisfied and bursting with pleasure thrashed about under her, pumping relentlessly until he collapsed onto the bed under her barely able to feel his limbs.

As his body hummed to a calmer state, he looked up to see Callie look down at him completely satiated and a realization overcame him and he needed her to know.

"I love you."

Callie froze, trying to take in the words he'd just said. She wasn't sure she heard him correctly, wondering if she'd imagined it because she was still a little foggy from flying high after what they'd just experienced.

Cade saw the puzzled look on her face as she tried to decipher what had just happened. One thing he noticed was the entire atmosphere in the room had now changed. He'd said something he'd never said to another woman before and though he wasn't sure what the impact would be, he felt good that he got the words out. He watched her slowly take the words in and he smiled when saw that they finally registered.

"I love you," he repeated wanting her to know that he said it the first time and he meant it.

"I love you too," she replied. "I love you so much Cade."

He kissed her, happy that they were on the same page.

"You're not going to run for the hills or anything are you? I'm not going to wake up and find that you've packed up and moved away am I?"

Callie winced as he withdrew from her body rolling her to his side so that he could draw her into his arms.

"I'm not going anywhere. I'm in this with you. I have never been happier than I am when we're together. I have to admit I'm not sure how this is going to play out in public. I know eventually it will have to if we're going to be a couple. I also know that I can't force us to hide from the public eye for a lot longer. For now, I want to continue to enjoy our love in private as long as possible."

"I promise, we'll figure this out. I don't want us afraid to revel in the love we share whether it be in private or in public."

"I know."

Cade pulled her close as she leaned into his chest exhausted and before long, sleep overtook them both.

22

Cade's cell phone rang early and he was glad he grabbed it before it woke Callie. They had spent the night at his condo after another marathon night of making love.

Two weeks after they declared their love for each other, they were still sneaking around like two teenagers who were trying to hide their love from their parents.

The day before, he had returned from a photo shoot in the Providence of Milan in Italy for the cover of the number one men's style fashion magazine. They were doing a full spread on him with some shots of him topless and working out to others that included him in business and casual attire. He rushed back to California to spend some time with Callie before taking off for a few months to begin filming his next movie.

He watched as she slept soundly while he couldn't seem to catch even a few winks. They'd made love all night barely getting any rest because they knew it would be a while before they saw each other again. He wanted her to consider visiting him on the movie set and she declined since their relationship was still undercover. They were concerned about the impact the time away from each other would have on the relationship but, confidently, she assured him it would work out. He wasn't as confident, but he would deal with it. He answered his phone seeing his brother Cameron's face flash across the screen.

"Cam, why are you calling me this early in the morning?"

"I just arrived in LA and I'm outside your door at the condo. I didn't know you would be here until I got here and saw your security out here. They won't let me up to your floor. What's going on?"

Cade knew Cameron wasn't going to leave so he checked to be sure Callie was still asleep and then slipped on pajama bottoms and told Cameron to hand his phone to Sean who was on duty.

"Sean, go ahead and let Cam up. I'll take care of it."

Cade looked around the room to be sure anything of Callie's wasn't in sight. He hated that after months of sneaking around, she still fought him on going public. Now that they had expressed their love for each other, he saw no reason to continue the façade they've been keeping up. A few moments later while he straightened up the room, he heard Cameron knock on the door. He opened it shocked to see Cameron and two of his friends from school. Anger rose knowing that he knew better than to bring anyone to any of his residences.

"Cam what are you doing here? You should be at school."

"I know, but I had a break and wanted to see you and hang out in California. I thought you'd be at your house so I was going to stay here at the condo. I've been calling you all night, but you wouldn't answer and I figured I'd be safe in coming here."

"Keep your voice down Cam." Cade nonchalantly looked toward the bedroom door.

Cameron followed his line of sight and sensed his brother must have a chick or two in the bedroom.

"Ah, I see someone had a wild night I bet."

Cade looked to Cameron and then to his friends who looked like they were itching for a story to sell to the press. He couldn't let on that Callie was there; it would crush her.

"Come on Cade, who is she? Some model, actress or just a groupie," Cameron asked.

Cade settled for a story that would involve a groupie. He was willing to spin any story that would make for a hurried exit for them.

"Yeah, she's nobody really. I met her a while ago and we've been kicking it for a minute now. As usual, with most women, she thinks there's more to this than there actually is, but there isn't. I'm just passing the time. You know how I do. I have to play the game to keep the panties dropping."

"I bet she's hot and phat in all the right places. Was she a wild one?" Cameron asked.

"Yeah, was she a wild one Mr. Weston?" one of the boys asked. Cade decided to play up his playboy image to placate the boys, hoping for a quick end to the conversation.

"She is definitely a wild one and knows how to make a man feel like a king. I barely have to do anything because of her zest to satisfy me."

The guys laughed and hooped.

"I told you my brother is the player of all players. They don't call him heartthrob for nothing."

"Keep your voice down Cam."

Cade tried to move them further away from the bedroom door.

"For what? If I know you, she's dead to the world exhausted from the workout I know you gave her."

"Is it someone we all know from a movie or television? I bet there's a story here," one of Cameron's friends said.

"No, she's just a woman like all the other women I know; she's nobody special. I'm heading out of the country to shoot a new movie and I don't keep long distance sex partners," he said.

**

Callie woke and reached over for Cade and all she felt was sheets and no warm body. She sat up, checked the time and knew it was morning, but where was Cade, she thought. She got up to go in search of him and when she reached the bedroom door, which was now shut, she could hear him talking to some guys in the main room. She didn't want to disturb them and turned to tiptoe back to the bed when she heard Cade describing the activities of a wild woman in bed.

Curiosity kept her at the door unable to turn away from the conversation. As she listened, she heard him talking about her as if she were some kind of groupie. Apparently one of the guys was his brother Cameron who she knew went to college in Florida. He was asking Cade all kinds of questions about the woman in the bedroom. Her heart dropped when she heard Cameron ask Cade if he would ever be serious about a woman. Since this was his brother, she assumed he would give him the honest truth. He once told her that he was close to his brothers and trusted them with everything. What she heard was disconcerting.

She heard him explain that he would never settle down with one woman. He felt that all women saw in him was money and status and their opportunity to get ahead. He explained how the woman he was banging now had big dreams and he believed she was telling him because eventually she would hit him up for some help to help make her dream a reality, but he was on to her and he would ride out the sex train as long as it lasted because when he was done with this one, there would be plenty more. The guys all laughed and so did Cade.

Callie wanted to cry. What she heard was that Cade has been playing her all along. He was using her until the next best thing came along. It didn't matter that a few hours ago, he'd professed his love for her as he had been doing for the past few weeks and now she knew it was a lie all to string her along. She turned to go towards the bed when she heard Cameron ask about the princess he'd been linked to lately. Cade explained that she was another side piece and he'd been tapping her for a long time and she was actually in town and he was heading over to see her later in the day to hit her off before she left town.

Callie couldn't take hearing any more of the conversation. She dropped the sheet, grabbed up her clothes that were thrown everywhere and quickly put them on. She put the few toiletries she'd brought with her in her overnight bag and went through the bathroom to the adjoining bedroom on the other end. She knew there was another exit from the condo through the kitchen which was the entrance his staff used. She slipped through the door which led to stairs at the end of the hall that a person could go down, but couldn't get up to the floor without a code for the door. She walked quietly to the door and as she was about to open it, she heard Aaron talking to Sean. Sean was explaining that Cameron had showed up with friends and was in the condo talking to Cade.

"Sean, why didn't you tell Cameron to go out to the house instead of bothering Cade. You know he hates being disturbed when he's with Callie. All hell is going to break loose later. You should have called me when Cam arrived."

She didn't wait around for the rest of the conversation. She opened the door and quietly closed it. She held her shoes in her hand and she sprinted down three flights of stairs until she got to the level where no passcode was needed. She found the elevator, got in and when she reached the front door, she grabbed a cab that was sitting there and headed for her hotel. Tears spilled down her face and all she wanted to do was go home; not just to the hotel, but home to Texas. California was not the place for her and maybe her mother had been right. Life in the entertainment industry was not for her.

23

Cade picked up his phone and called Aaron.

"Aaron, did you see Callie pass by you?"

After he returned to the bedroom after satisfying his brother and his friends' appetites for gossip, he looked around for Callie, noticing she and all of her things were gone. If she didn't leave through the front door, she must have gone out through the entrance his cleaning staff used. The flowers he'd brought her the night before were scattered across the floor and the three vases they were in were turned over on the floor.

"No I didn't see her and if she left by the back entrance, she did so real quiet like. Sean and I have been right here talking for about twenty minutes until Cam and his friends came out.

Cade was dumbfounded.

"I can't believe she would leave without saying anything. Maybe she got spooked when she heard voices and didn't want to be seen. This is starting to get ridiculous. She really shouldn't have left without one of you taking her."

"She didn't leave you a note or a text or anything before she left? She just rolled out?"

"No, I didn't get a call or anything from her. I don't even see a note anywhere. She just left and I've been calling her cell, but she's not answering. Something's wrong because she wouldn't leave without a word to let me know. I'm going to keep calling her to see if I can find out what's going on. Can you make sure the truck is ready if I need to leave?"

"You got it and good luck with Callie. Are you sure you're good?"

"I'm good. I'm just worried about her. She means everything to me and if something is bothering her then it's bothering me and I need to know what's going on with her."

He hung up from Aaron and as he hurriedly dressed, he dialed her cell over and over hoping she'd answer one of the calls. Just as he'd slipped his feet into his shoes, she finally answered.

"What do you want Cade?"

Her tone was angry and aggressive.

"Whoa baby, what's wrong? Did I do something? I came back to the bedroom, you were gone and the flowers I gave you last night were all over the floor. What's wrong?"

"You're really going to ask me that after what I overheard?"

"Callie, baby you're losing me. What did you

overhear? You have to talk to me and tell me what's going on. If something happened and I upset you, you shouldn't have left without talking to me."

Callie excited her cab and ran into her hotel to grab her things. While on her ride over, she was able to book a last minute flight out of Los Angeles and rather than go home to New York, she decided to go to her parents' home in Texas. She needed to get as far away from him and his lies. She had no doubt that once he found her gone, he would look for her and his first stop would be her hotel and she didn't want to see him; not after what he said about their relationship.

"Callie? Talk to me baby?"

"Don't call me baby!" she shouted, annoyed that he would still continue to play the game.

"Callie calm down and tell me what I did."

It was now or never she thought and she needed to get it off of her chest so that she could leave him and the relationship she thought they were having in Los Angeles.

"I heard you talking to your brother and his friends. I heard you dismiss the fact that you had any real feelings for me. I heard you put me in the category with all of the other women you've been bedding over the years as if I meant nothing to you at all, but someone you wanted to conquer like you've always been known to do. Once again, I've let myself be used and taken advantage of. The difference is I thought what we had was more than something casual. You played me and you lied to me. Is this what you do to get and keep women in your bed? You play some playboy game with their hearts in order to get what you first thought was unobtainable? Well I hope you got what you set out to get. I hope hurting me was worth the chase of finally getting me into bed and I hope you choke on that worth!" she shouted loudly walking through the lobby of her hotel. She didn't care that people were looking at her as she ranted like a lunatic.

She hadn't planned on talking to him before she left California, but she could no longer ignore his persistent calling and she couldn't turn her phone off in case anything changed with the flight out.

Cade didn't know what to say. He knew exactly what she'd overheard, but what she didn't understand was his reason for saying what he did.

"Whoa, Callie, wait a minute. I know what you think you heard, but that wasn't it at all. My falling for you wasn't a game or a chase or anything else you may think it was. It's more than that and you misunderstood what you heard me saying. Are you at your hotel? Stay there until I get there. We need to talk about this and I can explain everything."

"You have nothing to explain to me and even if you did, I don't want to hear it. I've heard enough and you make me sick. You got what you wanted and like I said, I hope it was worth it."

She didn't give him a chance to respond. Before he could get his next word out, she hung up the phone and entered her hotel room. She didn't have much to put together because she'd been spending all of her time with Cade either at his condo, his house or at the hotel near where the television series was being shot.

She was glad the show tapings had wrapped for a few days. She'd take those days to instruct her team with everything they needed to know because she had no intentions of returning right away. Based on the scenes for the upcoming tapings, the characters had already been styled and it had been logged so her team would know what to do in her absence. She needed to be far away from Cade and all of the wagging tongues she's sure would catch on that something happened and she once again would be the source of everyone's pity, something she was all too familiar with.

Angry didn't describe what she was feeling. Even though she was furious at Cade, she was angrier at herself because it wasn't his fault she let herself be drawn into his web; it was hers. She should have went with her first thought before she got involved with him, which was to say no and keep their relationship strictly business. He was good and she fell for everything he said to her and now she knew it was all just to get her in his bed. She felt stupid and humiliated and she hated herself for not sticking to her rule and vowing to never mix work with pleasure. Cade may be a snake, but she didn't have to fall for it and to top it off, she knew better. She threw what she needed into two suitcases and rushed out. When she reached the lobby, she let them know that she'd be checking out and asked for the hotel to have the rest of her things packed up and sent to her. After providing them with the address to ship her belongings, she went in the direction of the garage to get in her car. Her only focus was on getting to the airport and away from Cade.

24

Cade dropped his phone on the bed after Callie hung up on him. Now he knew why she'd disappeared on him. She'd overheard him tell his brother and his friends that she was nothing to him and that she was just some woman he'd seen and worked his ass off to get her in the sack. His brother then chimed in saying it was Cade's usual method of operation when it came to the women. He played along with them and said no woman would ever have his heart because he was the country's biggest playboy and if he fell to any woman's charms, he'd have to turn in his player's card. The conversation with them continued on like that, but what Callie didn't know was that he didn't mean any of it. He had a reason for what he said and he needed to explain things to her.

Cade knew he was in a big mess and wasn't sure

how he'd fix it. A knock at his door temporarily distracted him. He opened the door to find Aaron standing there.

"Hey, did you catch up with Callie yet? Where did she go?"

"Come inside," he said, not wanting the rest of the team to hear him.

Aaron entered and closed the door.

Cade paced back and forth trying to figure out how to explain his current situation.

"She's gone Aaron."

"What do you mean gone. Gone where? What's going on? She left and didn't say anything? How did she get by us?"

"Let me just say that I messed up in a very big way. Bigger than any screw up I've ever had."

He didn't want to talk. He needed to go and talk to Callie in person.

"Is the truck ready?"

"Yeah, it's ready. Where are you going?"

"I'm going to Callie's hotel to make her hear me out. I hurt her Aaron; I mean I hurt her bad and I need to fix it," he said opening the door and heading down the hallway with Aaron in tow.

"Cade, you have a production meeting in a few minutes for the movie. You can't miss this meeting and I'm sure whatever you did to Callie can be fixed later or tomorrow. You need to get ready for this meeting because you know Abby is going to be calling in a few minutes to be sure you're on your way."

He had no plans of going to the meeting until after he's had a chance to talk to Callie.

"I'm not doing anything until I fix this with Callie. I may have just ruined the best thing in my life and I don't care about a movie or anything else until I get her to listen to me. I need to apologize to her and then explain that it's all a misunderstanding."

As they reached the truck in the garage under the hotel they got in and neither said a word. Cade continued trying to dial Callie's phone and each time it reached the second ring, her voicemail came on letting him know that she saw it was him and forced his call to voicemail.

"I've never seen you like this over a woman before Cade. Are you going to tell me what's going on? You may as well spill it. The ride could take a while in this heavy traffic. What gives?"

Cade hesitated before spilling everything.

"You know my brother and two of his friends were here in the condo earlier. I tried to rush them back out before Callie got up. You know I trust my brother, but those fools he brought from school would have no problem selling a story of me and Callie to the media for the right amount of money so I told them it was some fly by night chick I'd been screwing and that she meant nothing to me. I played up the playboy image and I did it to protect Callie. I didn't want her name caught up in any gossip and his two friends looked like they were looking for something juicy to spill. Everyone knew my past with women so spinning a story with what the media already reports is nothing new. I thought she was still asleep, but it seems she wasn't asleep and she heard everything I said and it was brutal man. You know how I can be about women I pick up, but it's not like that with Callie. I love her man; I mean I really love her. I'm in love with her and I need her to understand the circumstance of the conversation she overheard."

"Dude, you don't have to tell me you're in love with Callie. I knew you were done for the moment you met her and I told you when you find that right one she'd turn your life upside down. It looks like you've found that one."

"Yeah and now she hates me and refuses to even talk to me. I don't care about any meetings or anything else right now. My plan is to stay at that hotel until she lets me explain. I need her to know that when I told her I loved her, I meant it. I wasn't playing her or saying things just to keep her in my bed. I said it because it's how I feel and I would never intentionally hurt her."

When Aaron didn't say anything, Cade looked over at him.

"Don't tell me you don't have anything wise to say at this moment."

"No, I don't. You're a man in love and right now you need to figure out how to fix this."

After what seemed like the longest car ride of his life, they had pulled up in front of Callie's hotel.

"Cade, you can't walk in the front door like you're not Cade Weston, the hottest star in Hollywood. You'll be seen by everyone and all hell will break loose."

"Not now because I don't give a damn about media, fans, paparazzi or nothing. All I care about is finding Callie and talking to her."

Aaron knew this was about to turn into a circus.

"Let me go in and have them call up to her room. You sit here in the truck and I'll see what I can do to get her to come down so that we don't cause a mad fan-fest out here," Aaron said.

Cade sat still and continued dialing Callie's cell while Aaron went inside. When Aaron returned, he saw a look on his face that said it was bad news.

"What?" he asked.

"She's not here man. Apparently while we were still at the hotel, she checked out."

"Checked out? Checked out where? Where could she have gone? The only people she knows out here is us and her staff on the set. You think she went to one of them, maybe Toni, one of her assistants? I know they've become really close and if she didn't want to see me, she'd go someplace I wouldn't be looking for her."

Without thinking, he called Abby.

"Abby, I need you to check with the production staff to see if anyone has seen Callie."

"Why, what's wrong?"

"We had an issue and she ran out on me. I've been trying to find her and she's nowhere. I checked her hotel and was told she checked out. I'm sure she knew I'd come looking for her there."

"Cade, you're supposed to be in a meeting right now, not chasing Callie around Los Angeles."

The last thing he wanted to hear was his assistant wearing her assistant hat.

"Not now Abby."

"Cade, listen to me."

"No, you listen to me. I don't usually raise my voice with you, but I'm telling you, ask everyone if they've talked to or seen Callie and call me back. I don't care about a meeting or anything else at this moment that doesn't involve you doing what I ask."

Abby knew what she was hearing.

"You're in love with her aren't you?"

"Yes Abby, I'm in love with her and I need to find her right now."

"Okay, I'm on it. Give me a few minutes and I'll call you back."

"Thanks and I'm sorry for shouting."

"Don't worry about it."

Cade hung up and waited.

**

Callie used her key and walked into her parents' home, glad that no one was around. She hadn't told them she was coming. She assumed they were still at work.

She was glad she was able to catch a last minute flight out home after leaving Los Angeles. Her mind was hazy with thoughts of hurt and betrayal and she needed to get as far away from Cade as she could. She couldn't believe how big of a fool she had been.

The words she heard coming out of his mouth were like a knife to her heart. Now she knew the answer behind his nickname, heartthrob.

His admission to his brother and his friends crushed her. Why she expected more or even something different from him she didn't know. She knew she was running a risk getting involved with a man who was known to have a different woman on his arm and in his bed every night. What was she thinking getting involved with him in the first place? Now here she was, crazy in love with a man who thought little of her.

She was drained and the only thing she wanted to do was lay down. She left her luggage in the living room and went up to her old room and threw herself across the bed. Visions of Cade was all she could think about and before she knew what was happening to her, she began to cry, softly at first and then unable to control the heartache, her body trembled with her cries.

"Callie? What's wrong? When did you get here?"

Callie was startled to sit up and see her mother standing in the doorway of her room. She tried to quash her cries to keep her from worrying, but the moment she laid eyes on her, she jumped up from the bed and ran into her mother's arms. She needed the comfort more than she needed her next breath.

"Callie, you have to tell me what's wrong. Are you hurt? Is someone else hurt?"

When her cries didn't simmer, her mother soothed her by rubbing her back and finally the cries that were racking her body were dissipating.

They walked over and sat on the bed.

"Are you ready to tell me what's going on and what prompted you to take a welcomed, yet unexpected visit home?"

"I've been a fool mom. I fell in love and it didn't turn out like I thought it would. The relationship wasn't what I thought it was and I allowed him to make a fool of me."

Her mother sighed with relief.

"This is about Cade Weston. You're in love with him?"

"Yes and he trampled all over that love by disrespecting me and the relationship I thought we had. It now seems I was in it alone."

"I have nothing, but time and we're here alone so why don't you tell me what happened and let's see if we can fix this."

"It can't be fixed mom. It's over."

"Callie, I already knew that you were in love with him. The way you talked about him when you called home leads me to believe you can make it through anything that happened. Now, start from the beginning."

Callie exhaled and told her mother what she overheard.

25

Cade was beside himself worried over where Callie could be. He'd had Abby check with everyone from the set and for three days, no one admitted to where she was. He had four days left before he had to fly out of the country to begin filming and so far he'd had no luck in locating her to explain the misunderstanding. He called her cell phone and had left several messages and she'd responded to none of them. He wasn't even sure she was listening to them. Each time he called, the phone went to her voicemail, never ringing.

He didn't try her again and instead called his grandparents to let them know he'd be out of the country.

"Nana! How are you," he feigned happiness. Although he was always happy to talk to her, he couldn't get his mind off of Callie.

"I'm doing great son. How are things in California?"

"Things are great. I'm calling to let you and Pop

know that I'll be out of the country for a few months. I'll try and fly in a few times over the next few months and I'll try to get home, but just in case I can't, I wanted you to know where I was and if you need something, reach out to Abby."

"Is this for that movie you told me about?"

"Yes. Taping begins in a few short weeks, but I'm flying out in a few days for pre-production meetings. How is everything at home?"

"Everything is great. Your grandfather and I are having some friends over later today for a card game. He'll be happy to hear you called. He's not here right now."

"That's fine Nana. Make sure you tell him I called."

"Cade, is everything okay? You sound strange. How is that lovely girlfriend of yours? I've been on cloud nine ever since you told me you were seeing someone and that it was getting pretty serious. Will we get to meet her soon?"

"I don't think so Nana. Right now she's not talking to me. I said some things that hurt her and now I can't get her to talk to me."

"What did you say to her? You men and your mouths," she exclaimed.

"I didn't say anything to her. She overheard me talking to Cam and what I said wasn't flattering, especially to her."

"Oh, no. I know how your conversations with your brothers can be. How bad was it?"

Cade breathed a sigh of disgust at himself.

"It was pretty bad. I didn't mean any of it. You know how I can be with Cam and Calvin and it got out of hand. I told you how she demanded that our relationship stay between the two of us. Well Cam showed up unexpectedly with some of his friends from school and I was with Callie. I didn't want to let on that she was with me or that it was someone I cared about. You know how everyone is always trying to sell a story. Cam knows better than to bring strangers around unexpectedly. It put me in a compromising position and so I held up the Cade Weston, heartthrob persona and said a few over the top things and Callie overheard me when I thought she was asleep and out of ear range."

"Oh Cade. You know how I feel about that heartthrob name and the person Cade Weston is in the public eye. That's not who I raised you to be and I know I didn't raise you to hurt a woman, especially one I know you care about."

"Nana, I know, but it was me trying to keep up my image."

"I don't care what you were trying to do, look at the outcome. Aren't you ready to stop playing up to that persona and be the person I know you are?"

"I'm more sorry than I can even explain to you. I love her and I would never intentionally hurt her. I thought she was asleep and I could throw them off by being the Cade they were expecting me to be. I was trying to hold up to my end of the bargain by protecting her."

"Cade, don't you dare throw this back on her!" she shouted.

His grandmother screamed so loud, Cade jumped as if he was again fourteen years old and she was scolding him for doing something wrong.

"I'm sorry Nana," he said giving in.

"I know you are. I expect you to fix this and besides that, I expect the next time you come home that you will be bringing her with you. I love you son, but I'm disappointed in you. Stop being Cade Weston and be Cade Lymon, the man I raised you to be. Cade Lymon wouldn't need to behave like this to impress anyone. That Cade doesn't get off on bedding one woman after another or living up to a name that's all visual and about nothing else. You are much more than that. Be the Cade who has fallen in love and is now hurting because the love of his life is hurting. Do better, be better and figure out how to fix this. I don't care what it costs you, but don't you dare leave this country until you have apologized to Callie and you know she's okay."

"I hear you Nana. I had already decided that film or no film, I'm not leaving until I see her to explain and apologize until she takes me back."

"Now, don't get me wrong, I'm upset with you, but she's no angel in this either. Don't you let a woman convince you to live in the dark. I don't care anything about your playboy image or her reasoning behind wanting you to keep the relationship a secret. Nothing survives if it only lives in the dark. Go deal with this and I expect a call telling me you have. I love you son."

"I love you too Nana. Tell Pop I'll call again before I leave."

Cade hung up and threw his cell phone on the seat beside him.

"Where are you?" he said out loud to an empty room.

"Where is who Mr. Cade?" Maria asked.

Cade turned and noticed her standing behind him as he absently-mindedly watched television. He retreated to his home so that he didn't have to deal with or talk to anyone.

"I'm sorry Maria. I wasn't asking a question. I was talking out loud without realizing it."

"You've been here for two straight days, the longest stretch without leaving in a long time. Are you feeling okay?" she asked coming closer.

"I'm feeling fine. I have a lot on my mind and I need the peace of this house in order to deal with it."

"Does this have anything to do with Ms. Callie? I wasn't intentionally listening, but I heard you leaving her a message on the phone last night."

"It's alright Maria. We had a misunderstanding and I haven't been able to reach her to try and explain."

"You also miss her a lot too Mr. Cade."

"Yes, I miss her a lot. I'm in love with her and I

don't want to leave the country without fixing things. I'm sure I can if she would talk to me."

"I'm happy and sad for you. I'm happy because I really like Ms. Callie and I like how she's brought out a side of you that we haven't seen before. I'm sad because you make a great couple and I see how unhappy you are not hearing from her. You still don't know where she is?"

"I tried everything. She's not at her hotel and the only people I know that she knows here in California either don't know where she is or are keeping it a secret because she asked them too. I know what that's like because I've been living it for months. I don't know what else to do."

"Did you try her friend, the one she called when she was staying here those days when she was sick? The same friend called the house number a few times as well. I gave her the number to call me if she wanted to check on how Ms. Callie was doing in case she was asleep. he number was a Texas extension and I'm sure it's still on the caller ID box."

Cade snapped out of his funk and turned to Maria with a huge smile.

"It never occurred to me that she would reach out to Angel. If she's here in California, Angel would know and if so, she's probably here with her."

He jumped up, kissed Maria on the cheek and ran for the kitchen phone.

Cade pumped his fist in the air when he saw Angel's number on the phone and dialed it.

"Angel, hi it's Cade."

"Hello Cade."

If he had any notion that perhaps Callie hadn't told Angel what happened, that thought went out the window the minute she said hello. He could hear the condescension in her tone.

"I apologize for calling you out of the blue, but I was hoping you would tell me where Callie was."

"Keep hope alive Cade because I'm not telling you anything. You hurt my friend and it's clear she doesn't want to hear from you."

He didn't push because clearly and understandably she was as pissed off at him as Callie was.

"Can you at least tell me if she's okay?"

"I'm not telling you anything. Do you have any idea how badly you hurt her? How dare you use her as just another play thing. She deserves better than that and she deserves someone better than you. She loves you and this is what she gets in return, to hear you demean her love for you and the relationship she thought the two of you were having."

"Angel, I know and I'm sorry for what she heard, but she didn't give me a change to explain. I didn't mean any of what she heard. I was playing up to the playboy image for my little brother and his friends. I was trying to throw them off of the trail of any kind of a serious relationship. I love her and I would never, ever hurt her or talk down to her or the love she has for me or what we have together."

"Have you tried to explain that to her?"

"I tried, but she was so angry, she wouldn't hear me out. She hung up and hasn't taken my calls since. It's been three days and I'm worried about her. I promise you, I was not playing with her or her feelings. I think I fell in love with her on that plane ride from New York to California and that love has grown stronger every day. I need to find her and explain. More than anything I need to see her. Help me out here. Is she still in California? My next move was to fly to New York to her apartment to see if she was there."

He waited for what seemed an eternity for Angel to respond. When several seconds went by, he thought he had not convinced her of his true feelings for Callie.

"She's in Texas. She went home and has been there for the past few days. She's at her parent's ranch. I swear if you don't fix this I'm going to cut off your heartthrob balls and feed them to my dogs!" she exclaimed.

Cade smiled.

"I promise I will fix this and thanks for the visual."

"Yeah, well, I have a few more if you hurt my friend again."

"That's never going to happen again. Thanks for

helping me out."

"Are you coming to Texas?"

"I'm already on my way."

26

Three days had passed since Callie had shown up in Texas with the weight of the end of her relationship with Cade casting a shadow over her happiness. Her parents and her sister tried to soothe her, but nothing worked. For three days she'd wandered around not knowing how to pull herself up out of her misery. No matter what happened between them, she loved him and that love wouldn't go away no matter how much she thought about how he'd hurt her. She knew the only thing that would soothe her would be to do something she did when she was younger whenever something bothered her; she needed to ride her favorite horse and spend some time at her cabin in the woods.

When she was a teenager, instead of having a tree house, her father built her and her sister separate small cabins on the edge of their property. She loved her cabin and the serenity it provided her whenever she spent time there. She was glad the staff kept the cabins cleaned and stocked with linens even though she rarely came home.

She gathered everything she would need for a night in her cabin and headed downstairs. At the foot of the stairs she encountered her father.

"Hi Dad."

"Hey baby girl. It looks like you're going up to the cabin."

"I am. I'm going to take Dolly and ride her out. I'll probably stay the night so don't worry if I don't come back tonight."

"Take food with you or I can have one of the ranch hands bring you something later."

"I'll take some with me."

"Are you feeling any better?"

"A little," she lied.

"I swear if I lay my eyes on that Cade Weston, I'd pound him in the ground for hurting you."

"You will do no such thing. I'm a big girl and I can handle my own big girl problems. Thanks for being concerned, but I'm fine."

"Okay, make sure your phone is powered up and call if you need anything."

**

Cade's limousine pulled up to Callie's parent's ranch. He looked around amazed and impressed with its size and beauty. He was nervous when the limousine pulled up to the gated entrance to the property, but after a few words and a call to what he assumed was the house, he was allowed in. He wasn't sure he would be after announcing who he was.

He exited the car and was met by a man who looked like photos of Callie's father that she'd shown him.

"Mr. Weston."

Cade was greeted with a handshake, but no smile.

"Mr. Hurston, sir. It's a pleasure to meet you."

"So you're the schmuck who hurt my baby. Star or no star, that's my baby."

"Yes sir, that would be me, the schmuck. Let me first apologize to you for what happened. I never meant to hurt her and I came here today to talk to her and hopefully explain. Would it be possible for me to talk to her?"

"I don't think that's a good idea after what you've done."

"Leave that young man alone," a voice from behind Callie's father said.

Cade looked around him and saw a beautiful older version of Callie walking toward them. No doubt it was Callie's mother.

"Hello Mr. Weston," she said coming up to him extending her hand.

"Hello Mrs. Hurston. I'm sorry to intrude and please call me Cade."

"You're not intruding."

"Yes he is."

Callie's father was serious and Cade knew he was being protective as he should be. One day when he has a daughter, he knew he would be the same way. He never thought about having children until he'd fallen in love with Callie. Now he wanted that more than ever.

"Hush up and invite him inside."

Cade didn't move, waiting for the invitation.

"Follow me son and you better have a good explanation for why my baby girl ran home to us crying her eyes out."

Cade didn't speak, but followed them into the house. Once inside they gathered around the dining room table where he was invited to sit.

"Now, we don't want to pry, but Callie told us what happened from her perspective and without too much detail, we'd like to know what happened before we allow you to talk to her. She's very upset and I know it's because she loves you and even after what happened, she still does, but she's hurt."

"Mr. and Mrs. Hurston, let me first tell you that I love Callie very much and I never, ever meant to hurt her. She overheard me saying some things to my brother and a few of his friends and though they were mean and harsh and totally disrespectful, they were not about her or any other woman. I was being the Cade they knew and I didn't want them to suspect that Callie was there and that I had feelings for her. We had been doing everything to keep the relationship private to protect her and her ability to make it as a stylist on her own without the drama of being connected to me. I didn't mean any of it and basically I was acting. I tried to explain everything to her, but she hung up on me and now won't take my calls."

"So you really do love her and haven't been using her all this time?"

Cade looked her mother in the eyes when he replied.

"Yes, I really do love her more than anything and I would never use her. I can't say that I haven't been that kind of person in the past, but not since I've met her. Callie is my world and I don't care how long it takes or what I have to do, I plan to make it up to her and prove to her that nothing in this world is as important to me as she is. I need to talk to her and explain and I'm hoping she will hear me out."

"You understand how things have been for Callie trying to make a life in the entertainment industry. We don't want to see her hurt, used or abused and if you say you love her and you really mean it, then we have no objections to you seeing her while you're here," Mrs. Hurston said.

He looked to Callie's father knowing he needed his approval also.

"She's right son. My daughter loves you very much and I can see you are sincere in your feelings for her, especially after you flew all the way here. She went horse-back riding. It's the one thing she's always loved doing that relaxes her. She rides out to a small cabin that I built for her years ago. She went up there to relax and spend the night. Do you ride son?"

"No sir. There weren't many horses where I grew up."

"I'll have someone drive you up the mountain to the cabin that she calls her sanctuary which is on the edge of our property. If she's not in the cabin, she's probably about a half-mile down a path that you can see from the cabin; it's right on the water. Good luck and I hope it works out for you both. It's also nice to finally meet you. We've seen all of your movies and enjoyed them. You're a great actor. Do me one favor and leave the acting side of you here in this house. Give her who you really are and I have no doubt things will work out."

"Thank you sir."

**

After the car dropped him off, Cade told the ranch hand that he could leave and if Callie refused to forgive him, he deserved to have to walk back to the house.

He checked the cabin and she wasn't inside. He followed the path that led away from the house and a few minutes later, he saw her and her horse at the water's edge of a beautiful lake.

He walked up to her and spoke before he reached her, so that he wouldn't startle her.

"Do you know what I had to go through to get

here?"

Callie turned at the sound of his voice and stood quickly.

"What are you doing here Cade?"

He came closer.

"I came for you. You left the condo, hung up on me when I called you and then stopped taking my calls. I checked your hotel, but you'd checked out and then after I had Abby check with everyone on the set to try and find you, I had to resort to being scolded by Angel before she told me you were here. Luckily Maria remembered Angel had called the house and we still had her number."

"So now I guess everyone on the set knows that we were sleeping together."

"No Callie, they don't. Abby was very discreet in her inquiries and never gave on that she was asking for me. Can we stop playing dodge with everyone? I don't want to do that anymore because doing so is why we are where we are right now, both hurting."

"You hurt us Cade, not me."

"I know that and I came here because you wouldn't talk to me and let me explain myself."

"How did you get past my family?"

Cade chuckled at the interrogation he received.

"Your parents chewed my ass off and after I explained my side to them and convinced them that I was sorry for what you heard and that I loved you, they had a ranch hand bring me up here."

He waited, but got no reaction from her. Still he

smiled because he'd missed her and angry at him or not, he loved her and he wouldn't be any place other than with her at this very moment.

"Well I don't know what you told everyone, but I don't want to hear it, so you need to turn around, jump back on your jet and go home. I have nothing to say and you have nothing to say that I want to hear."

"Are you sure about that Callie? I mean, you haven't given me the chance to say anything about that day. You hung up after you said what you had to say, but I think you're being unfair not allowing me to explain."

That got a rise out of her. He watched as she put her hands on the hips he loved grabbing a hold of as he made love to her and turned her head to the side to look at him as if he were speaking in another language and she couldn't understand anything he said. Even angry, she was the most beautiful woman he'd ever seen. He smiled at her attempt to be angry at him.

"What are you smiling at?"

"I'm smiling at the woman I love. Just because you're angry at me doesn't mean I don't love you. It doesn't mean that I'm not still very much in love with you because I am."

"Stop it Cade. You know nothing about love and from what I heard, you can't possibly expect me to believe you're in love with me. The only person you're in love with is yourself."

"Will you stop being angry for a minute and let me explain, please?"

When she didn't respond he continued on.

"I'm sorry you heard my conversation with my brother and his friends. I know how it sounded, but that wasn't what it was. I know what I said and I meant none of it."

Cade could see she was about to interrupt him, but he stopped her.

"Let me finish before you dig into me."

She stopped whatever was about to come out of her mouth and let him continue.

Cade walked right up to her with only a whisper of a space between them. When he came close, he noticed that instead of looking up at him, she turned her face to look away from him. He knew he wanted her to see his sincerity as he spoke, so he reached out and turned her face back around so that she was looking right up into his face. Her beauty took his breath away, but he needed to focus on fixing his relationship.

"Baby, listen to me when I say to you I love you. What you heard was a story I made up so that they would leave and not know that you were who I had in the bedroom. They showed up and when I went to let them in, I forgot our clothes were strewn all around the living room. You remember that night don't you?" he said softer while caressing the side of her face.

She didn't respond so he continued getting the

rest of the explanation out.

"I love and trust my brother, but I know nothing about his friends and if they'd known that the woman I had in the bedroom was you, the woman I love, I have no doubt they would have tried selling the story to the highest paying magazine or news outlet in Los Angeles. I can't get my brother to understand being careful about opportunists. The only way I could think of to keep you out of it was to make up a story that would go over on them. They had already seen our clothes everywhere and I wanted to protect you. I know what you've been through in the past and I didn't want that for you. I made that story up and it did the trick. They exited right after that. I swear I didn't mean to hurt you and I certainly didn't play any games or tricks to get you in my bed. You were there because first I care about you and second because I love you baby."

"The things you said though were horrible. I've never heard you refer to any woman that way."

"I know and I'm sorry. If I haven't learned anything, I've learned how hurtful treating women as if they don't matter can be to a woman. Being who I am, I've never given it a second thought before. I've never felt for a woman the way I feel about you and I'm sickened by the things I said. I'm sorry, not just that you heard it, but that I said it even though I know I didn't mean it. We've talked about my history with women and that is who I was, it's not who I am now. I never thought

I'd fall in love with anyone because every woman I encountered wanted something from me whether it was to be associated with me for fame and fortune or because they wanted to be the one to try and tame Cade Weston. For the first time in my life everything I have achieved in my career means nothing unless I'm able to share it with you."

Cade paused and rubbed his finger across her face wiping away the tear that fell from her eye.

"I haven't been able to eat, I've barely slept and I've put a lot of things on hold because I can't let you walk out of my life as if our time together meant nothing. Every second I've spent with you from the first moment we met at the airport has meant the world to me and I don't want to go back to my life without you being a part of it. I feel complete when you're in my arms. Not talking to you and being with you these past few days has been torturous. I know you're angry with me and I hope you believe what I'm saying right now because it's the truth. I don't care how long it takes, I'm not leaving here until I know our love is back on track. I mean it when I say nothing in this world matters to me if I don't have your love anymore. Your love gives me life and Aaron predicted what my life would be like when I met the one. The one for me is you and you know that's saying a lot. You know the life I lead and for the first time in my life, I've met a woman who didn't want to be with me because I'm Cade Weston. I met the woman that I could simply be Cade with and I can't let that go. I'm in love with you baby and I can't live my life without you. Don't make it so that I have to."

He waited before saying another word. He saw tears pooling in her eyes and he hoped they were because she still loved him as much as he loved her. As the tears rolled down her face, his heart melted a little more. He never wanted to see her cry unless they were tears of joy.

Slowly he leaned forward giving her the chance to push him away if she were going to and when she didn't, he kissed the tears from her cheeks, first the left, then the right.

"Don't cry baby. I'm sorry for putting you through this and I promise if you give me the chance I'll make sure I never, ever hurt you again."

Callie's heart melted from his words and the love she still carried for him. She looked up at him as she spoke.

"I've spent these past few days wondering why you would hurt me and why you would play me. I wondered if you did it because of what you knew about my past knowing that I'd mixed work with relationships before and you used it as an opportunity to get me in bed. That conversation with your brother and his friends played over and over in my head and each time the impact was worse."

"Callie, none of that is true and I can promise you nothing like that will ever happen again. I'm all yours if you'll have me and I promise I will do anything to make it up to you. Give us a chance to get back to the love we've been enjoying. This time I want to do it out in the open; no more hiding. I don't think our relationship can survive the secret anymore. I want everyone to know I love you. Do you love me baby?"

Callie didn't hesitate.

"Yes, Cade, I love you very much."

"That's everything to me right there. I've never had that kind of love from a woman before and I know you mean it. I know there's no ulterior motive behind your love and that's the kind of love I realized I'd been missing in my life. I don't even want to know if I'd ever find this kind of love again because until my dying day, I intend to love you and love getting your love in return."

Callie reached up and placed her arms around his neck as he drew her near.

No more words were spoken as the kiss they both yearned for consumed them. Poured into the kiss was all of the love they'd been sharing and had missed out on the past few days.

"This is forever sweetheart," he said before leaning down and kissing her again letting her know that she will never regret giving them a second chance.

The kiss was hot and fervent and before long they equally felt the need to be closer.

"Can we go back to my cabin? I want you to

show me how much you've missed me. You have some making up to do," Callie said, purring with need.

"Does the cabin have a bed or at least a blanket. The way I need you right now, you're going to need a soft surface."

"The cabin has everything we'll need."

"That's all I need to know."

Cade led the way as he joined her hand with his as their slow paced turned into a sprint to get naked.

Epilogue
Eighteen months later

All of Hollywood turned out for the biggest award show of the year. The who's who of the industry were already walking the red carpet where cameras flashed, snapping the elite in their finest. Cade and Callie were a few car lengths away from the limelight and she was more nervous than she had been a few months ago at her wedding to Cade.

Their wedding was the event of the year and everyone from A-list stars to friends she'd grown up with were in attendance. Though everyone speculated that their wedding would take place out of the country or at some exclusive spot that only the most rich and famous used, she was glad when Cade agreed to having their wedding on her parent's sprawling Texas estate.

Acres of their property were turned into a wedding wonderland. They'd had a huge tent erected for the ceremony to keep paparazzi out and invitations and transportation for guests were done at the last minute to keep all aspects of their plans as much of a secret as long as they could.

Besides the wedding tent, they had another giant tent set up for the reception where they hosted over four hundred guests. Everyone had enjoyed a great day of celebrating the new life she and Cade were planning to have together.

Though the road to getting to where they are now was a rocky one, it was well worth it and Callie couldn't be happier.

"Are you ready for tonight, Mrs. Weston?"

Callie had been distracted by the bright lights when his words interrupted her thoughts.

"I am a little nervous. I've never walked the red carpet before. What happens if while I'm walking I fall flat on my face? That would be embarrassing and my behind could be spread across the tabloids by the morning. That wouldn't be a good look for me," she kidded.

Cade leaned over and planted a sweet kiss on his wife's lips, trying hard not to smear her perfectly applied lipstick.

"You're going to be fine and you're not going to fall. I've seen your ass and I find nothing about it embarrassing. In fact I'm thinking about it right now and if I don't soon stop, I'll be the one embarrassed when I exit the limousine with a boner," he laughed.

She laughed also and laughing is exactly what she needed to calm her nerves. She smiled when he pulled back and saw the naughty look on his face.

"Don't even think about it. It took me hours to

get ready for tonight and even as a stylist I wouldn't be able to fix myself up if we did what I know you're thinking about. Change your thoughts to the weather or something else because you're not getting anything until we get back to the house tonight."

"Do I get something extra special if I win the award?"

"Baby if you win, you can have anything you want and since I already know you're going to win, let's just say the entire night is yours for the taking."

When he reached for her, she slid to the other side of the limousine.

"Don't even think about it. If you smear or wrinkle anything before I get to my seat, you're sleeping on the couch tonight," she smirked.

Cade threw his hands up in surrender.

"Okay, I know. The theme for tonight is don't touch. I hear you, so I'll keep my hands to myself as long as you know all bets are off the minute we get back to this limousine in a few hours."

The limousine pulled up to the entrance to the red carpet and now was their turn to walk it. While they waited for their door to be opened Cade did pull her a little closer to him.

"Baby, I want you to know that this night is not only special because I'm nominated, but I've come to realize that until I'd met you, my life wasn't as perfect as it is now."

Callie was as ecstatic over their happiness as he was.

"Thank you for coming for me that day at my parent's house and for fighting for us."

Cade took her hands in his and kissed them since her lips were off limits.

They sat back and waited for their turn to exit the limousine.

Callie thought over all they'd been through and it was well worth getting to where they are. They had been the talk of Hollywood since the announcement that they were in love followed by their extravagant wedding. As usual the media hype tried to make their coming together drama-filled, but any skepticism about their love was calmed when people saw the love that blossomed between them. No one could doubt that they were deeply in love. The backlash that Callie thought would happen never surfaced. She went back to her life as a stylist while he left the country to work on his movie and tonight was the epitome of all of his hard work since he was nominated for best actor and the movie was up for best picture. He was still on top and with her own line coming out soon, she was following her dreams.

**

Callie and Cade lay in bed looking at his award for best actor that sat on the shelf on the wall in front of the bed. Callie had the shelf added while they were gone knowing that when they returned, they would have the award to sit on it. She had that kind of faith in his acting ability.

"Congratulations again on that award. I knew you would be coming home with it," she said as she snuggled up closer to his naked body. Her hand roamed all over him, unable to resist touching his gorgeousness. She knew she would never tire of looking at him.

"Did I tell you Asia reached out to me to ask if I could get a read for Mateo for your next production?"

"No you didn't tell me, but I'm hoping you told her where she could stick her favor."

Callie laughed heartily.

"I sure did. Can you believe the games she tried to play by spreading rumors that the reason I was fired from the New York series was because I tried to get ahead by sleeping my way through the producers and director, not to even mention that I went after Mateo behind her back?"

"Yeah, little did she know that I already knew all I needed to know about you and I wouldn't believe any of that mess anyway. That's childish behavior in an adult arena. I'm surprised she even contacted you after she found out we were involved and getting married. She must be pretty desperate now that the reality show was cancelled."

Callie shook her head in agreement.

"I hear Mateo's career is pretty much over since those pictures came out of him with the studio president's wife. He's not coming back from that."

Cade turned to her, pulling her into his embrace. Callie was still amazed that this man was hers and all hers. She looked forward to many years of being his wife.

"What's next for you now that you've won over every heart in the industry this year?" she asked.

"I have several offers I'm looking at for starring roles, but I think the next offer I want to take on is being husband to you and hopefully father to our children."

Callie looked up at him hoping he was talking about sooner rather than later.

"Are you serious Cade? Don't play with me because you know there is nothing I want more right now than children. I wasn't sure you wanted children right now since we've only been married less than a year."

"Baby, I know that and I before I met you I thought my life was complete. Now I can't wait to see your belly swell with my son or daughter and if you're ready, I'm more than ready. I plan to take a much needed respite and let my money make more money while we take some time enjoying us. We didn't take a honeymoon because of all of the press for the awards show, but now that it's over, I want to take some time and focus on us. Having this career is fine and I appreciate being named heartthrob of the year which added to the additional offers for roles coming in, but for the next year at least, I am all yours and we can go anywhere and do anything you want to do."

"Are you sure Cade? I know that's a major sacrifice for you and I know what your career and business ventures mean to you."

"They mean nothing if I don't put you first."

She leaned up and turned to him to drive her point home.

"Do you know what I really want to do? I want to do something unexpected. I want to build our home away from this Hollywood madness in Texas on the land my father gave us. I want it to be a place where we can escape from all of this and get some quiet time. I want our kids to know about raising animals and horseback riding and all of the other things I learned and loved growing up in Texas. Is that too tame for you?" she asked.

"I'll tell you what, baby, tonight I want to spend all night making love to my beautiful wife and start working on expanding our family and in the morning, I'm going to have our bags packed and after I call your parents to let them know we're coming to stay for a while, I'm going to get the jet ready and we're going to Texas to begin working on plans to build that house on our land. I'm going to let all of the business that I've built all these years make money for me while I take some much needed time to enjoy my life with you and I can't think of a better place to do that than on the ranch."

Callie loved the sound of that.

"What do you say to having your grandparents come to the ranch for a visit while we're there?"

"I think it's a great idea. I'll also tell Cameron. He was planning to stick around here for a few days since he came out for the awards show. He needs some time to chill and get away from the limelight in Hollywood. He could use some down time in Texas before classes start back up. I think he's beginning to like it here and putting a little normalcy back into his life will be good for him."

"That sounds good. The more the merrier and my mom will be happy to have all of these people for her to cater to."

Cade slid further down in the bed, pulling her along with him as he reached over to dim the bright lights in the room.

"Speaking of catering to, I want to cater to your wants tonight and I intend to spend the whole night doing it."

Not letting her speak, he leaned in and sealed his lips to hers invading her mouth with his tongue which was hot and heavy with need to mate with hers. As the kiss turned wild, he slid her under him and just when he was about to slide into her, his cell phone rang.

"Damn," he bellowed. "I thought I turned that off. Let me shut it off before it rings again."

Cade reached for it and glanced at who would call him at this late hour. His body stiffened when a text message appeared on the screen and he saw the code that appeared. It was a code that he, Cameron and Calvin had created that meant the there was an emergency. The first four digits of the code were the same for all of them, but when it was followed by the number eight, he knew the emergency was Calvin. Something was wrong. He quickly sat up and dialed the satellite phone that he'd provided for both of his brothers to reach him at all times no matter where any of the were in the world.

"Cade, what's wrong?"

"I don't know. It's Calvin and something's wrong. He sent me a text to call with the emergency code and the number he called me from was his satellite phone. We only use those in case of an emergency and after all these years, this is the first time he's used it."

Callie got right up, grabbed her gown, pulling it over her head before coming around to his side of the bed. She sat next to him as he completed dialing the number.

"Calvin?" he asked when the line picked up.

"No this isn't Calvin, this is Mason one of Calvin's friends. There's been an accident and Calvin's been injured. I'm not supposed to call you because we were on a secret mission, but Calvin gave me this information to reach out to you if anything ever happened to him."

Cade's heart stop beating as he waited for more information.

"How bad is he?"

"He's pretty bad. The military is flying him back to the states for medical care, but I want to warn you, his injuries are pretty severe."

"Tell me where they're sending him and I'll meet the carrier."

"That's not a problem, but that's not the only reason I'm calling you."

"There's more?" he asked.

"Let me explain as much as I can, but then I'll need to hang up. I'm not supposed to tell you this. Calvin was in the middle of a mission to rescue a woman from her family, who are powerful in the drug business. In the midst of the rescue Calvin was injured, the woman was killed and so was her brother and his men. Her father survived and has gone into hiding. The woman's child survived and no one knows about the baby except me. I have some friends looking after him, but I need to get him out of Colombia and on American soil."

There was a pause and Cade was losing patience.

"What are you not telling me Mason?" he asked nervously.

"The baby is Calvin's son Cade. The woman and Calvin had been seeing each other secretly for a year and when her father learned that she was pregnant by an American, he had her kidnapped."

"A baby? Calvin has a baby and the mother was killed?"

Callie heard it all, got up and began packing a bag for Cade knowing that as soon as he got off of the phone he would be leaving. She picked up the house phone and called Aaron on his cell.

"Aaron, Cade is going to need the jet tonight. I don't have the destination yet, but he has a family emergency. As soon as I have the destination so that the pilot can file a flight plan, I'll call you back, but in the meantime, can you get him up and at the airport? He needs you and Sean here immediately."

She hung up the same time that Cade disconnected his call.

"I'm packing you a bag and Aaron is getting your plane ready. What else happened?"

Cade got up and started dressing in the clothes she'd laid out.

"The short story is Calvin was injured rescuing a woman he'd been having a secret affair with. During the rescue, she was killed, but the baby survived. He's a three month old boy named Camico and Mason, the guy who called, is getting the baby safely to this country. He's texting me the information on where they are sending Calvin. I'm going to finish dressing. Check my phone and when he texts the information, call Aaron and give it to him so he'll know where we're going. I need to get to the hospital when they bring Calvin in."

"What about the baby?" she asked.

Cade stopped in his tracks. He has a nephew who was alone and he needed to get him.

"Mason said it would be a day before the baby

gets to the states. I don't know what to do about him yet. I have to think it through. It's a baby."

Callie knew.

"When the baby arrives in the states, send the jet to pick him up and bring him to Texas to the ranch. I'll look after him while you look after your brother."

"You're the best baby. Call Cam for me and get him moving. Tell him we have a family emergency and Calvin needs us."

**

Follow Calvin's story in *Heartbeat*, Book 2 in *A Lovers' Heart Series* in 2016.

Navy Seal Calvin Lymon was injured in the line of duty and now needs around the clock care to get him back on his feet. The days of therapy that drain him are nothing compared to the steamy nights of passion with Ava Cortez, the nurse who provides care in more ways than one, that are having the biggest impact on his ability to get back to reality.

Can he risk giving his heart to another woman while at the same time, protecting his son from a family that wants him back?

COMING NEXT MONTH FROM CHERYL BARTON

AUGUST 2015

AMOROUS OCCUPATIONS: THE ELECTRICIAN

The party invitation said everyone had to wear a masquerade mask the entire night, a New Orleans tradition.

Dara Marshall couldn't resist the opportunity to spend an uninhibited night of passion with National Football Association coach Nelson Riley, the guest of honor, knowing that her identity was hidden by her mask.

Dara's world turns upside down when she discovers the gorgeous coach is the newest client of her father's business and after she's sent on a job at his condo, she does everything in her power to not give away the secret of who she is.

Nelson could never forget the sexy temptress he'd spent an unforgettable night with, even when she tries to hide behind a mask and baggy overalls.

***Enjoy this excerpt from
Amorous Occupations: The Dancer by
Cheryl Barton – Now available in
paperback and for your e-pub device***

Max tried to remain calm as the dancer came toward him in the seedy New York night club where he knew no one would recognize him. He was sure his dark attire and the baseball cap sitting low on his head that partially covered his face shielded his identity from anyone who wasn't standing directly in front of him.

He never thought he'd be in a place like this where men came who needed relief from their home lives which consisted of wives and children who placed demands and pressures on them daily. He had neither a wife nor children, but tonight the darkened club with a dozen or so sexy women clambering about trying to entice men and women out of their hard earned money all for a few lap dances, provided the fantasy he needed to do what he came to the club to do.

Max watched several women as they gyrated around the club going from one hand that held out money to the next, hoping to entice a few into something a little more personable. Unbeknownst to them, he wasn't there to get a lap dance. He had other plans in mind for the dancer who was slowly making her way over to him. He'd been trying for several nights to get her attention and had high hopes that tonight would be the night that she'd tune into the signal that he was interested.

As the music played loudly and the liquor poured non-stop, Max sipped on his beer and waited. He didn't have to wait too long once the dancer made eye contact. When he didn't look away, he assumed she thought she had him. Little did she know, she was the one being had.

When she finally reached him, he remained calm, but the rapid tapping of his right foot told another story. He looked at how she was dressed in a hot pink thong, very high heeled clear stilettos and nothing else. He looked at her breasts and could see that she wasn't a very voluptuous woman, but her shape was perfect for him and for how he needed her to look. The familiarity was perfect.

Max let his eyes travel up and down her body as she sashayed around for him making sure he could see her from every angle. When she turned around, showing him her backside, his heart skipped a beat. Now that her face was turned away from him, in his mind he could imagine her looking like anyone he wanted and when the face of the woman he wanted her to be flashed before his eyes, his body jumped with anticipation.

Tonight was finally the night, he thought to himself. He could barely contain his excitement over how the night could turn out. Now that the sexy little vixen was finally about to give him some attention, he knew that his patience had paid off. As she turned back around to face him, coming right up to him he knew it would be the perfect night, at least for him. This time was a long time coming from when he first began his search for the right woman. Max knew she had to be perfect and after not getting the joy and excitement from the first few women he lured in, he had a feeling this one was what he'd been looking for.

Max had come to this place several times, scoping it out. His first visit was to check out the place and to see if any of the women looked like his Shelly. He'd been to several places like this one around the city in hopes that one would resemble the love of his life. An unwavering exhilaration resonated throughout his body the moment he spotted her on his first visit.

The dancer looked so much like his Shelly that they could pass for twins. As the days went by, Max knew that she may be able to pass for Shelly in the looks department, but her dance moves were not up to the standard of Shelly's, who was a professional Broadway actress and dancer. Tonight that fact didn't matter much to him since it wasn't her dancing skills he was interested in.

Steadying his legs as she came up to him became a task as she leaned over so that her naked breasts were mere inches away from his face. Not wanting his nervousness to scare her away, he never took his eyes off of her face, giving her an even, intense stare. It was her face that became the draw and the obsession for him. She had the same beautiful, flawless face as Shelly, though she wore more makeup than he liked. Her long weaved hair flowed down around her shoulders in a cascade of loose curls that he couldn't wait to grasp tightly in his hands. If he thought it wouldn't draw attention to them, he would reach for her now, but he needed to wait. The time for that was getting closer.

"You're watching me," she said in a soft, sultry voice.

Max's body stood at attention.

"Since you came up to me, I assume my watching you intrigued you," he responded.

He was hoping they wouldn't waste a lot of time conversing because he knew it would draw attention from others in the club to them, something he didn't want.

"Well, what will it be tonight handsome?" she asked.

"Not something I can get sitting here."

When she didn't immediately respond, he knew she was thinking about what was obviously a subtle proposition.

"Where would this something you'd like to get need to take place?"

"Well sweetness, it depends on you and what time you get off."

"Well, I'm not really allowed to leave with the customers; it's against club policy."

Max went in for the kill to make sure she changed her mind.

"Well I have a thousand dollars that says your club policy is null and void tonight."

The mention of that much money got her attention when he saw how wide her eyes widened.

"You have a place near here big spender?"

"Not real close by but I have a car that can get us to my place in no time at all and have you back here at the club in time for your stage time in two hours," he replied calmly, not giving away his anxiety.

"How do you know I have stage time in two hours?" she asked.

"I've been coming here for a few nights and you always have the twelve-thirty a.m. time slot for your show. Right now it's only ten and I can guarantee you that I'll have you where you belong by your show time. I'm so riled up for you sugar that I'm sure things will happen quicker than I'd like, but as soon as you need. What do you say to that? Is a thousand incentive enough for you?"

Max knew he was pushing, but if he didn't make his move tonight, he wasn't sure he'd get another chance. He could see her running the options through her mind, contemplating what she could do with the thousand dollars. He was sure from looking at the clientele, that she'd never make that much money from one customer and in this case, she wouldn't have to split it with the club.

"I could get in trouble and even lose my job if the boss knew I was leaving with a customer, especially one that may spend money in the club tonight."

Max had the answer.

"I'll tell you what I'll do because I really want to spend a little alone time with you. I'll head on out of here, making sure I'm not seen, while you go make an excuse of some type of an emergency, telling your boss you'll be back in a couple of hours just in time for your show. I'm sure you can persuade him to see things your way," Max said, making sure he looked her over from head to toe, letting her know that he meant for her to use her femininity to get her boss to go along with it.

"If I do this, how do I know you actually have this thousand dollars?"

Without any hesitation, Max reached into the inside pocket of his jacket and pulled out a stack of one hundred dollar bills. What he didn't let her see was that only the first five bills were hundreds, while the others were one's, but she was so focused on the hundreds on top and how thick the stack was, that she didn't question him further. He didn't show the money too long, afraid she might catch on so he quickly placed the bills back in his pocket.

"Proof enough for you?" he asked.

"What kind of car do you drive?"

"It's a black Mercedes. I'll pull around the corner so that no one coming in or out of the club will see you get in it. I'll be in it ready to drive off as soon as you get in."

The pull of a thousand dollars for an hour or so

with a customer was too big of a take for her to turn down and Max knew it.

"Give me twenty minutes," she said before turning and walking away.

Max got up, pulled his cap further down on his head to block any view of his face and exited the club. Once outside, he wasted no time getting behind the wheel of the Mercedes he'd stolen a few hours ago from a hospital garage. He'd watched the doctor as he showed up for work, knowing it would be hours, until the doctor's shift ended before he noticed the car was gone. By then, Max wouldn't have a need for it anymore.